W9-AXA-016

MASTERS

OF

MINECRAFT

The Invasion

by Terry Mayer

Copyright © 2014 Terry Mayer

All rights reserved.

ISBN-13: 978-1495417863

ISBN-10: 1495417867

I dedicate this book to my son Jack, who inspires me every day.

Previously in Masters Of Minecraft

Twelve players have been dragged, kicking and screaming into the world of minecraft to compete in a tournament to find the one true master of minecraft.

So far, three players have died in the tournament. First to die was Darknight, killed by his own hand when he attacked Jethro Skybuilder only to find that he lost the same life points as the player he attacked. This fact is only known by Nathan the Noob and Jethro Skybuilder.

Second to die was Captain Sparkles; drowned in a flooded mine after a giant tidal wave covered the whole of minecraft.

Last was Sky, infected by a zombie virus he was unfortunate enough to be outside at sunrise and was consumed in a ball of flames.

Jay, his younger stepbrother Jack and his friend Nathan have been taken into the game against their will and have so far fought a massive tidal wave, a zombie virus infection, and an attack by creepers. As the first book ended, we found these three had teamed up with Jethro Skybuilder and Natasha and were escaping from a massive attack by creepers.

Four other players are also battling it out to find the ultimate player, but as of yet we do not know who these players are.

The creator of minecraft, Notch, has also been dragged into the world by his own creation, Herobrine. Not knowing what is required of him we were left at the end of the first book with more questions than answers.

So starts book two in the gripping Masters of Minecraft Series- The Invasion.

Players

1. Jay Lightningbuilder

2. Jack the Dweeb

3. Nathan the Noob

4. Jethro Skybuilder

5. Natasha

6. ~~Darknight~~

7. ~~Captain Sparkles~~

8. ~~Sky~~

9. Unknown

10. Unknown

11. Unknown

12. Unknown

Chapter 1

Run, don't look back

After running for the last two hours, the five survivors crouch behind a low wall overlooking a small village.

"So what do you reckon Jay, is it safe?" asks Nathan.

"Nowhere is safe, but sometimes we have to take a chance. What do you think Natasha; shall we give it a try?"

"I think me and you should head into the village and check it out, the others can stay here so if trouble breaks out they can either rescue us or at least get away."

"Good idea, Jack, you take the others over to that small wood over there and watch our backs, any sign of trouble give one of those loud whistles that drives mum nuts."

"Ok Jay, come on guys, it will be dark soon and we have to make a decision one way or another." Heading off across the field in a crouched run, they make it to the woods unnoticed and signal an all clear to Jay.

"Right Natasha, you ready to do this?"

"Ready as I'll ever be."

Heading into the village at a quick jog, they make it to the first house unnoticed and stand with their backs to the wall.

"Right Jay, you head into this house and I've got your back."

"How come I have to clear the house?"

"Because I've already cleared one village so that makes it your turn, you cool with that?"

Remembering how Natasha and Jack had cleared a whole village in search of seeds to make a cure for the zombie virus for himself, Nathan and Jethro, he sheepishly nods his acceptance.

Right, on three, two, one, go, go, go.

Running to the front door, he kicks it open and with sword raised, charges inside to find two zombies standing in the corner. Immediately they sense fresh meat and turn in his direction. Bringing his sword about in a wide swing, he slices the heads from the zombies and they both fall to their knees.

Hearing the all clear from Jay, Natasha walks into the house and takes in the scene. "Right, search for anything useful then we can do the next house."

"Searching cupboards, Jay looks over his shoulder and remarks."Got a better idea, why don't we just run from house to house and open all the doors and let the zombies out."

"Because there could be too many to fight and then we'd be zombie chow you dork."

"Yeah, even in the sunlight? Not so smart now, eh?"

"Well, never did say I was the brains of this outfit now, did I?" she laughs. "Good idea Jay, you ready to give it a try?"

"Lets do it, we don't have much sunlight left."

Running from house to house they kick open the door, shouting at the shambling figures as they run. Soon quite a hoard have stumbled from the shadows are are in various states of death as they burn in the sun. As the last house is cleared, Jay remarks. "Not the brightest bunch, are they?"

"Hey, don't knock it Jay. If zombies actually had brains, we would be in some serious trouble here. Get the others, this place will have to do, it's as good as anywhere else we have passed."

"Agreed," replies Jay walking to the edge of the village and signaling the all clear to the others.

*****

Chapter 2

War Room

Sitting in the war room, or in this case, what passes for the village pub, they discuss their options.

"I say we make a stand here, it's small enough to defend, but large enough so we are not too close to the walls," announces Nathan.

"I don't know Nate, we will never defend any place against creepers, not with the numbers we saw this morning. I still think Jay's original idea to head to the coast is the right one," replies Jethro.

"Yeah, it could work Jay," joins in Natasha.

"But guys, we've been running for hours. The coast is nowhere in sight. I don't know about you but I've never been in a biome that just keeps on going. I don't think there is a coast here at all."

"Yeah, and it's getting dark. If there are as many zombies around here as there were last night, we will never make it. We need to hole up until morning."

"Agreed, right Jack and Nathan, you're in charge of building walls, two blocks high around the entire village. Jethro and Natasha, start digging a singlewide tunnel to that small hill behind the village. That's our escape route if the creepers arrive tonight. Use whatever you dig out to build the walls so you can keep your inventories full. Right, let's move, we don't have long."

"Uh cool Jay, but what are you going to do while we do all the work?" asks Jack sarcastically.

"Little brother, stop worrying about me. I'm going to search the village, see if I can find anything valuable, now go."

Jumping up they all run off to perform their tasks as Jay sets off searching each house in turn. In the fourth house he finds a chest with a couple of iron ingots and some bread. In the fifth, he collects a few pumpkins and a chest with meat stored in in. Great, at least we can all eat and replenish our health, and with the iron and seeds, we can make some more zombie virus cure.

Removing his crafting table and furnace from his inventory, he walks around the village looking for some sand. When he finds some, he digs up four cubes, puts it in the furnace with some wood, and makes four glass blocks. Laying two of the blocks on the crafting table, he combines them with an iron ingot to make a large syringe, and then fills the syringe with zombie flesh and seeds creating a cure for the dreaded zombie virus.

With his tasks completed, he heads back to the village pub when something catches his eye. Walking towards a small decrepit looking house, he wonders how he missed it when he cleared the village. Drawing his sword he kicks open the door and rushes into a small single room that is empty apart from a large table. Cautiously checking under the table, he turns to leave when a small, shrunken creature lands on his back and starts tugging at his hair.

"Get off me you witch," he screams, grabbing her robes and throwing her across the room.

"Witch, who are you calling a witch?"

"You, you old crone."

"I'm not old, I'm only fourteen. Well I was when I got here anyway."

"What do you mean, we've only been playing for a few minecraft days, if you were fourteen when you got here then you still are, duh!"

"Duh yourself, fool. I've been here forty years or more. I've lost count."

"What! But that's like, 200 odd earth days!"

"Like I said, I think I'm still fourteen, but hang on. Two hundreds days would make this about March, so what do you know, I'm actually fifteen."

But how can you have been here for that long. We only just arrived?"

"You're not the first to arrive here and no doubt you won't be the last."

"There's others? Great, where are they, maybe we can work together and get out of here?"

"Dead, every single one of them."

"Crap, so what happens to them when they die?

"No idea but I didn't want to find out myself so here I still am."

"But your parents must be looking for you?"

"Yeah, so what do you suggest, I just kill myself and see what happens, hope for the best?

"No, I wouldn't."

"Damn right you wouldn't. There's no guarantee that we go home after being here, wherever the hell here is, so I am not killing myself."

"Ok, ok, I got it. Sorry I brought it up. By the way, the name's Jay," he says holding out his hand.

Eying him warily, the old crone steps forward and pulls back her hood revealing a fifteen-year-old girl.

"My god your human!"

"Yeah, I usually get that reaction."

"But we're all block men. Why are you human?"

"Don't know, but I think I was one of the last humans to arrive before you all became Steve's."

"So have there been a lot of humans here?"

"Dozens over the years, but they have always been evolving. When I arrived, quite a few others were here already but no one lasted very long against the mobs. Then these blocky characters started arriving. Not quite like you but not like me either, but they would usually get killed pretty quickly, then I guess the first Steve arrived a couple of years ago and even though none have survived they last a lot longer than anything else."

"How come?"

"Well, for starters you have this inventory thingy inside of you. Man that would be so helpful, and you can build things so quickly either on the crafting table or just by placing blocks."

"Yeah, that is pretty cool," he smirks.

"Great for you Mr cool. Not all of us can do that."

"Sorry, so what is it with this place, why is everyone coming here?"

"The Masters of Minecraft tournament. It's all been a test, readying humans in preparation for this tournament."

"But who is running the tournament?"

As she is about to answer a shout comes from outside.

"Jay, where are you bro. We've finished the walls, what do you want done next?"

Looking back at the girl Jay sighs, "duty calls, you better come with me and meet the rest of the gang."

✱ ✱ ✱ ✱ ✱

Chapter 3

Who Are You?

Back at the pub, they all surround the girl and ask question after question until Jay shouts for silence.

"Come on guys, she can't answer you if you keep firing questions at her. Jethro, you start."

"Right, nice to met you young lady. My name is Jethro Skybuilder, and you are?"

"Hailey, nice to meet you Jethro."

"Nice indeed. Before we start let me introduce you to everyone. This is Nathan, Jack, who is Jay's brother and this is Natasha. Right, introductions out of the way, maybe you can explain what in good god is happening?"

"You have all been invited to play in the Masters of Minecraft tournament, that you know, but what I don't know is why Nathan and Jack are here?"

"What do you mean?" asks Nathan.

"Well, for years this world has been in preparation for the tournament and a list of players was announced a few weeks ago, but Nathan and Jack were not on the list."

"How was it announced?"

"In the sky. A list of twelve players printed across the sky and the voice read them out, but like I said, you two were not on it."

"They weren't invited. They were holding onto me when we teleported, or whatever it was, and were dragged in. Nate here hasn't even played minecraft before."

Looking at Nathan, Hailey gives a little smile. "Tough break kid, not the best circumstances to learn how to play."

"No, not the best," replies Nathan with a shrug. "So, who was on the list?"

"Right, there was Jay Lightningbuilder, Natasha, Jethro Skybuilder, Sky, Captain Sparkles, Darknight, PowerGlide, Warlord999, Munster, Lenno Lenno, PowerMad and Notch."

"Notch is here? Shit, well I guess that rules him out as the person running this game."

"No, it's not Notch that runs this world it's ...." As an explosion detonates outside Hailey, is stopped in mid sentence.

"Quick everyone, outside, sounds like the creepers are back."

Running out of the pub, they head to where the explosion had ripped a hole in the wall surrounding the village. Ducking through the opening Jay expects to see hundreds of creepers advancing on their position but is shocked to see nothing. Just empty fields.

"Looks like it was a lone creeper. Guess we just got lucky but seeing the hole left by just one creeper I think we better build some more defenses. Before it gets too dark I suggest we dig a trench around this village, two blocks wide and at least four two blocks deep, more if we have time. Use the cobblestone to build a two block high wall behind the trench. Hopefully, that will keep the creepers away from the village. Hailey, watch our backs. Ok, let's move."

Running from the village, they all head in separate directions and start digging. Work goes quickly and it's not long before a deep trench with a low wall is built all around the entire village.

"Nate, Jack, run over to the tree line and place some torches, Jethro and Natasha same thing behind the village. I'll do the wall, now go."

As the torches are placed, the area is lit up like a supermarket car park, allowing a clear line of sight even as the sun starts to set.

Gathered behind the low wall the friends stare out over the field, wondering if they will make it through the night.

"Uh Jay, this fortification is great and all but I think we need a plan in case the creepers arrive," stammers Jethro.

"I've been thinking about it for the last hour Jethro. In theory the creepers won't be able to get across the trench to blow up the wall but not all of the usual minecraft rules seem to apply here."

"Like what?" asks Nate.

"Well Nate, mobs can't come out in sunlight or they burn but those creepers attacked us during daylight. In addition, that flood should not be possible, but it happened. It's almost like we are playing in somebody's hacked game, modified to suit their own purposes."

"And what purpose would that be?" asks Jethro.

"Your guess is as good as mine Jethro but it looks like this whole world has been designed for one reason, the tournament."

"Yeah, but designed by who?"

"Herobrine."

All heads turn in the direction of Hailey.

"Herobrine brought me here so I assume he brought you too."

"But Herobrine is just a myth, or at the most a hacked mod pack."

"Maybe that is how he started but I'm telling you, it was Herobrine who brought me and every other human here. I haven't seen him since the first Steve turned up but I'm sure he's responsible."

"Who is Herobrine?" asks Nathan.

"Herobrine started as a hoax. Players started saying they had met a mysterious character in the game that sometimes attacked them, and then some wise ass built a mod pack including Herobrine. I know Notch wasn't too impressed when the rumor went around that Herobrine was his dead brother, because he removed the Herobrine 'bug', his words, from later releases of Minecraft."

"Ok, so he's this invented character, so how could he have brought you here Hailey?" asks Nathan.

"Hey, don't look at me like I'm mad."

"Well it is a little hard to believe that an invented character brought you here."

"What, and you think this is normal?" she replies pointing to the village and then each of them in turn.

"Touché my dear, you are of course quite right. This is all very strange, quite unbelievable, so if you say Herobrine brought you here then who are we to doubt you."

"Thank you Jethro. It's nice to know that at least one of you has some common sense," she replies, glaring at Nathan.

"Ok, ok. Calm down people. We can discuss this later, right now we have company."

Pointing out across the field a dozen or more zombies shuffle from the woods towards the village. Reaching the trench, the first zombie simply keeps walking and falls straight in, followed by the rest.

"Uh, pretty dumb or what!"

"Yeah, but a least they have tested the trench for us and it seems to be working. Right I guess there's no sleep tonight, luckily we don't seem to need it so...."

"Talk for yourself, I'm still human and have human needs," chirps in Hailey.

"Sorry, forgot. Right, all us Steve's," smiling he looks at Hailey, "will be up all night. We need to police the trenches. If the mobs get past them we need to fall back to the village, if all else fails we use the escape tunnel and make a run for it, just like before. Any questions?"

Everyone shakes his or her heads.

"Right, let's spread out, shout out if you make contact so we know what's happening but try to stay in your own area. We can't afford everyone fighting in one place then getting overrun from behind."

"Uh Jay, I think I've got a better idea."

"Really Hailey, well I guess you better tell us then," Jay replies sarcastically.

"Why don't I go up in the tower, I'll have a clear view of the whole village from there and I can direct you all to the trouble spots. That way if someone needs help I can send some but can still keep an eye on their zone so we don't get blindsided. So, what do you think Jay?" she asks with a little smile playing on the corner of her lips.

"Got to hand it to you Hailey, it works. Ok everyone, Hailey is now in charge. She will direct you where you are needed so listen out for her, ok?"

Everyone nods his or her agreement.

"Right, let's go. Good luck guys, hopefully this has all been for nothing but I've got a feeling that we are in for a long night."

★ ★ ★ ★ ★

Chapter 4

The Invasion

Creeping through the shadows the group moves stealthily towards the village. A loud snap of a breaking branch assaults PowerGlide's ears and he spins around and glares at the group. "Quiet you fools, if they hear us we are done for," he snaps.

"Sorry boss," replies Warlord999.

"Just keep it down, we're right at the edge of the village. This is where it gets a little dicey. You all know the plan, when it all kicks off we make our move. We all ok with that?"

"Sure boss, whatever you say," replies Warlord999.

"Good, then let's get in position, anytime now the proverbial shit is going to hit the fan."

Moving forward once more, they spread out behind the trees that surround the small village and prepare themselves for what could be their last stand.

*****

As darkness draws in, more and more zombies stumble towards the village, only to fall into the trench.

"There must be a couple of hundred of them down there now. Are they thick or what?"

"Yes Jack, they are stupid creatures but I for one don't want to get too close to them. Once being a zombie was quite enough," replies Jethro.

"Oh sorry Jethro, I forgot you were a walker only this morning. So, how did it feel to be brain dead?"

"I guess it probably felt like being you Jack, the only difference is I was cured, what's your excuse?"

"Ouch Jethro, that really goes deep," replies Jack, grabbing his chest and staggering around.

Laughing, Jethro replies. "Yes, I quite like that, but seriously, it's not something I would wish on my worst enemy."

"Yeah, well I'm just glad we were able to cure everyone."

"Yes indeed, and may I say thank you once again for your sterling efforts."

"We're cool Jethro; you would have done the same."

"Yes of course, but maybe..." looking around Jethro pauses in mid sentence. What is that noise?"

Listening, Jack strains to hear but whatever Jethro can hear is too far away for him. "Man Jethro, you either have killer hearing or you're imagining things."

"Shush, it's getting louder. I think you better go get Jay."

"Really? What is it Jethro?"

"Go Jack, quickly."

Returning shortly both Jack and Jay run over to Jethro.

"What do you hear Jethro?"

"Listen Jay, it's getting louder all the time."

Cocking his head to the side Jay listens to a low rumble. "Sounds like thunder in the distance. You think we are due a storm."

"Oh yes Jay, I think a storm is approaching but it's not rain that I'm worried about. I think that's the sound of hundreds of creepers."

As the sound grows louder and louder Jay turns to Jethro. "I sure hope you're wrong because there must be thousands of creepers to make that much noise."

As the noise increases to nearly deafening levels they stand on the wall watching a dust cloud descend on the field, then suddenly, silence.

"What the hell?"

"Just wait Jay, I think this is it."

As the dust starts to settle, the scene in front of them comes into view.

Staring out over a field of moving bodies, thousands upon thousands of creepers just stand looking at the village in absolute silence. Then with an unheard command, they rush forward in one huge wave of destruction.

"Get back," shouts Jay, jumping from the wall. "Get away from the walls, the creepers are attacking."

Explosion after explosion rips through the night, throwing a dust cloud into the air, but amazingly, the wall stays intact.

"What's happening, why are they exploding?"

"Look!" exclaims Jay, pointing at the tower where Hailey is firing flaming arrow after arrow into the creeper hoards. As each flaming arrow hits, the creeper starts buzzing and explodes, setting off a chain reaction and starting the next creeper to buzz then explode.

"My god, she's going to wipe them out single handed."

"No such luck, look, they are retreating."

As they watch, the creepers withdraw out of arrow range and mill around the edge of the village.

"What are they doing? I didn't think creepers worked in any sort of organized way."

"They don't usually, but nothing is normal here. What's that on the hill Jay, your eyesight is better than mine."

"Crap!"

"What is it?"

"I don't know, but whatever it is, its bad news. I saw it yesterday when we were under attack at the castle but I hoped it was just some creature that happened along but I think it's commanding the creepers."

As the dust once again settles, the creature on the hill comes into view. A huge dark shape, blacker than the night stands ten blocks high. Although silent, it waves its arms in the air and appears to be communicating with the creepers who immediately start to shuffle towards the village again. They stop just out of arrow range and start running on the spot, all four feet raising dust into the air.

★ ★ ★ ★ ★

"Ok boys, this is our chance, just as discussed, get in and get out quietly, now move."

Creeping from their hiding place at the edge of the woods, they run, crouched over, towards the rear of the village. At the trench, they reach into their inventories and remove cobblestone, placing it quickly over the trench. As soon as the first section is bridged, Warlord runs across with his pickaxe in hand and starts knocking down the small wall. The other three continue to place cobblestone blocks over the trench until a wide section has been covered.

"Hey Munster, tell Warlord to move onto the village wall, knock an opening then get the hell out of there. Keep your eyes open, we don't have time for a skirmish. PowerMad, jump down in the trench and make some steps up into the village. We'll get the zombies to do our dirty work."

Jumping into the trench PowerMad quickly starts a cobblestone staircase leading directly to the village. At the same time Warlord and Munster, pickaxes in hand, quickly knock two large openings in the village wall, keeping a keen eye out for the other players.

As Munster reaches ground level, he calls out to PowerGlide. "Boss, the stairs are done but the zombies are right behind me, better make a move unless you want to join the fight."

"Quiet you fool, don't you ...." he is stopped in mid sentence as an arrow slams into his shoulder and sends him tumbling backwards.

"Invaders, everyone, invaders at the rear of the village, the wall is breached," shouts Hailey from the tower, notching and firing another arrow, this one hitting Warlord in the leg as he tries to escape over the bridge.

"Run, our cover is blown. Head for the rendezvous point, move out," screams PowerGlide, wrenching the arrow out of his shoulder. "Munster, give Warlord a hand with that arrow."

"Yes boss," he replies, grabbing the arrow in his leg and snapping it off, eliciting screams from Warlord. "You're welcome, now move your ass or you're on your own."

Running from the battle, with arrows raining down behind them they look back and see the first zombies coming up from the trench and heading into the village.

"That should keep them busy," laughs PowerGlide, darting into the forest, heading for the rendezvous. "Nothing like a little mob help to win this game, suckers don't stand a chance now, attacked from both sides at once this should all be over before morning."

✱ ✱ ✱ ✱ ✱

Hearing the commotion Natasha runs towards the rear of the village and arrives at the wall just as the first zombies attack. Pulling her steel sword from her inventory, she cuts down the first two but is quickly overwhelmed by the sheer numbers advancing on her. With two holes in the wall, zombies are pouring in and threaten to cut off her escape if she waits much longer. Turning to flee, a hand grabs the back of her head and holds tight. "No, not a chance I'm going out to a zombie," she screams, swinging wildly with her sword, cutting down two more zombies advancing on her, but she is still held fast. Zombies fall to Hailey's arrows as they climb through the holes in the wall, causing a temporary obstruction, slowing the flow into the village, but Hailey cannot get a bead on the zombie attacking Natasha, the angle of the tower being all wrong. Jumping around to stop the zombie from sinking its teeth into her neck Natasha continues a slice away at the advancing hoard, but realizes that her time is running out as she feels the sharp pain of zombie teeth slice into her neck. "Noooooo," she screams, grabbing the zombie by the head and throwing it off her, running from the advancing hoard as arrows continue to rain down she heads towards Jay at the front of the village.

★ ★ ★ ★ ★

Pulling out his sword Jay turns from the wall overlooking the creeper army as he hears Hailey's shout her warning, but just as he prepares to leave the creepers surge forward in several places, with dozens throwing themselves into the trench. As they detonate, huge areas of the trench explodes with craters. Still running on the spot, raising dust, the creepers appear to regard the damage before another dozen or so launch themselves into the trench, causing more explosions.

"OMG, creepers aren't supposed to be clever!" exclaims Jethro.

"Why, what's so clever about blowing yourself up?"

"Look Jay. They are not simply killing themselves, look at the holes they are making."

Looking through the rising dust clouds Jay peers into the murky depths of the trench, suddenly realizing that the trench is no longer very deep. The explosions have brought down the sides of the trench wherever they met sand, and formed a slope up to the low wall.

"Clever buggers, I've never heard of anything like this before."

"The only time I've ever heard of anything like this was years ago, on a server I used to play, when someone added 'The Invasion' mod pack. That made all the mobs attack and destroy your dwellings, but I never heard an announcement this time, like when 'The Infection' mod pack started. "

"Well maybe the first announcement is the only announcement. Maybe it was just informing us that mod packs are now in play."

"Sounds reasonable, so we had better be alert for any eventuality. If any mod pack can come into play at any time, without warning, this game has just got a whole lot harder."

"Jay, Jay."

Turning they both see Natasha running straight towards them holding her neck.

"Jay, quick, I need the... ugh."

"What? Natasha, what's wrong."

Moving quickly Jack tackles Natasha to the ground and wraps his arms around her. "Quick Jay, she's been bitten, give her a zombie cure."

"What, how was she bitten?"

"Jay quick. I can't hold her forever."

Reaching into his inventory, Jay removes a syringe and plunges it into Natasha's leg. Almost immediately, she stops fighting and her eye's start to clear.

"Thanks Jay, uh, you can get off me now Jack."

"Right, sorry," says Jack, releasing Natasha from his bear hug.

"Don't be sorry, you just saved me and I'm forever in your debt."

"Yeah, yeah, well done Jack, but Natasha, how were you bitten by zombies, did they spawn inside the village?"

Suddenly remembering what happened to her, she jumps up. "Damn, some players breached the defenses at the rear of the village and let in a whole heap of zombies, come on, quick."

Just as she turns more explosions rip through the night.

"You and Jack go; me and Jethro are staying here. Take this with you, it's the last one." Throwing the last syringe of zombie cure to Natasha, she catches it and dashes off.

"Thanks Jay, come on Jack, we've got zombies to kill."

"Great, here we go again."

✸ ✸ ✸ ✸ ✸

Running back in the direction she had just come from they find Nathan standing in a two block wide opening between the houses fighting an increasingly large hoard of zombies.

"Natasha, I can't hold them. Build a wall quick, we have to close off this part of the village."

Seeing that Nathan is right, she reaches into her inventory and retrieves some cobblestone, then places it in the gap between the houses, 2 blocks high. "Jack, close off those other houses, Nate, on the count of three, jump back and I'll block the opening, ok, one, two, three." As Nathan jumps out of the way, she quickly places 2 blocks of cobblestone, completely blocking the opening. "Good word Nate, quickly now, let's help Jack close off any other buildings, looks like we're making our last stand right here."

✸ ✸ ✸ ✸ ✸

Turning back to the wall Jay looks out at the creeper army and shivers. "What are we going to do Jethro? It's not going to be long before they manage to climb up out of the trench then it's just this tiny wall, which won't stop them more than a couple of minutes."

"Cobblestone! This wall is made of cobblestone, if all things remain the same, and I'm not saying that they will, but it might just work."

"What will work?"

"Cobblestone Jay!"

"What the heck are you talking about Jethro; you're not making any sense."

"Sorry Jay, I do that when I'm excited. In the normal minecraft game, creepers can only blow up one cobblestone block at a time. So if that remains true, then all we need to do is thicken this part of the wall and it will take dozens of creepers to get through."

"Yeah, but just in case you haven't noticed, there are thousands of them out there," he says pointing out at the creeper fields.

"Yes, of course, but we have the advantage. Only one creeper can attack each section of the wall at a time or they just blow each other up. If we are quick, we should be able to repair some sections before the next creeper arrives. Now quickly, start building another cobblestone wall inside of this one."

Reaching into his inventory and removing cobblestone Jay starts building another wall as fast as he can. "Jethro you old dog, I thought you said you only played on creative mode? Where did you learn these tricks?"

"Dear boy, just because I like to build does not mean I don't understand the fascination of survival mode. I played it for many months on many different servers, I used to be quite efficient at it too," he replies smiling.

"Efficient? Where on earth do you come from Jethro? I've never met anyone who speaks like you."

"Later dear boy. If we survive this night I will regale you with my story, but for now, build as fast as possible as I suspect we are about to get company."

★ ★ ★ ★ ★

"Right, that should hold them for a while. Jack, you stay here and guard our rear. I don't think those other players will be back but let's not take any chances. Nate, you come with me, I think Jay and Jethro could use a little help."

Rushing to the forward defenses, they find Jethro and Jay building cobblestone walls. They quickly explain their plan and both Natasha and Nate join in building.

"Look out Jay, here they come," shouts Hailey from the watchtower.

"Thanks for the heads up Hailey. If any get through this wall, it's your job to keep them busy while we retreat to the village."

Just as he finishes shouting his instructions the fist creeper makes it to the top of the slope, starts to fizzle and throws itself against the wall. An ear-shattering explosion nearly deafens the defenders, but as the dust settles, it is clear that Jethro's idea is correct.

"Look, only one block destroyed. You clever bugger Jethro, this might actually work. I'll repair it," Jay shouts dashing towards the wall.

"Wait Jay. Let them attack the wall first, let's not show our hand just yet. Everyone, build a step so you can climb onto the wall then get your cobblestone ready. On my mark run forward and repair the wall closest to the trench, then work back as quick as you can. If a creeper comes at you get off the wall quickly."

Watching the creepers attack the wall, Jay quickly realizes the genius of Jethro's plan. As each creeper makes it to the top of the slope and detonates against the wall it blows just one block of cobblestone but also takes out two or three soil and sand blocks below itself, so destroying their own slope and slowing the attack from the next creeper. After over 200 creepers have detonated, either destroying wall sections or just trying to repair their own slope Jethro gives the word and all four dash forward, jump onto the wall and start placing cobblestone blocks as fast as possible. Nathan is the first to retreat as a creeper runs at his section of wall and detonates. Shortly after the other three are also forced to abandon their positions.

"So, how'd you all do? I managed to place 24 blocks," asks Jethro.

"28 for me."

"Only 22 for me, sorry," replies Nathan.

"46 at last count."

"Wow! Jay Lightingbuilder strikes again. Way to go Jay!"

"Thanks Natasha. So we repaired 120 blocks, and their trench is caving in, making it harder to build ramps. We might just have licked them, what do you think Jethro?"

"I don't know Jay. It all seems a little easy. There are thousands of creepers against us. I get the feeling that things are only just getting going."

As Jethro finishes his sentence, multiple detonations sound from the rear of the village.

"Jay, the creepers are coming in through the rear, over the bridge," warns Hailey from the watchtower.

"Have they breached the walls yet, what were the explosions?"

"No, they are still outside, I just shot a couple, and they blew each other up."

"Way to go Hailey. Ok guys, same plan as before, let's build some more walls."

Rushing to the rear of the village, they start thickening the cobblestone walls that Jack is guarding.

"Jack, build cobblestone walls, quick before the creepers get here."

"Sorry Jay, I'm all out."

"Me too," shouts Jethro. "Has anyone got any left?"

"Here, take some of mine," replies Natasha, throwing 64 cobblestones on the floor and turning back to the wall she is strengthening.

Grabbing half each, Jethro and Jack head off in different directions to help with the wall.

"Ok everyone, gather around. We now have a wall 6 blocks thick. Who has any cobblestone left?"

"I've got 4."

"None."

"Me neither."

"I've got 10."

"Right, 14 blocks, and I've got 4, so 18 in total. That's not a lot to defend this place. Jack, Natasha, and Nate, take 6 blocks each. You're in charge of repairing the walls. Steal some from other sections if you need to, just do not let the creepers in or we are finished. Jethro, come with me."

As the others prepare themselves for the creeper assault, Jay and Jethro climb the stairs of the watchtower.

★★★★★

Chapter 5

The Last Stand

Gazing out over his surroundings, Jay is shocked at the sight that greets him. Thousands upon thousands of creepers fill the surrounding fields and at least five hundred zombies are milling around at the tree line.

Gasping, he splutters. "We're doomed. Where the hell did they all come from?"

"Spawned in hell by that thing," replies Jethro pointing at the huge black creature directing the battle from the top of the hill.

"What is that anyway?" asks Hailey.

"No idea, but you can bet your bottom dollar that it has something to do with Herobrine. It's no coincidence that it's here and trying to kill us."

"So, what do you think Jethro, what's the next course of action?"

"Die, more than likely, old chap," he chuckles.

"Nice, thanks Jethro. How about you Hailey. You've been here longer than any of us, what do you suggest?"

"I say let's take the fight to them!"

"WHAT!" Both Jethro and Jay splutter, not expecting that answer.

"Exactly! They will never believe that we will do anything other than sit here and die, so I suggest we attack them. We burst out of the village, strike the creepers with flaming arrows or spears, then when they explode.."

"But they won't explode just because we set them on fire."

"Of course they will Jay, just like when I shot them earlier, they exploded and set each other off."

"But that does not happen in minecraft."

"But it does here, and that's all that matters. Right, as I was saying. We burst out of the village and set as many on fire as possible, as they start exploding they will detonate each other, and in such an enclosed space this whole place is going to go up in one huge explosion."

"Nice Hailey, but I never really saw you as they type to go out in a blaze of glory."

"Neither do I Jay, and that's why I have a second part to the plan," she replies with a cat like smile playing on her lips.

"Ok, don't keep us in suspense Hailey."

"Right, the moment we have all thrown our flaming spears and shot our arrows, we run back into the tower, down the tunnel and hot foot it out of here. When the village explodes we can escape in the confusion."

"Nice plan. It might just work. How about it Jethro, you on for a little detonation party?"

"Well dear boy, it certainly sounds a lot more appealing than my idea now, doesn't it?"

"It surely does. Right, let's fill the others in, we don't have much time."

Just as Jay utters these words the first creeper explodes against the cobblestone defenses below, followed shortly afterwards by yet more detonations.

★ ★ ★ ★ ★

"Ok guy's, on the count of three, two, one, move it!" screams Jay above the deafening explosions.

They all jump up onto the low walls, using a block they placed previously, and throw their flaming spears as far into the creeper hoards as possible. Each has two quickly constructed spears and some make shift sharpened torches. From above, Hailey lets loose a barrage of flaming arrows, striking one creeper after another, and setting them fizzing and bumping into each other.

"Now!" screams Jay as he jumps from the wall and dashes into the tower. Running in swiftly behind him are Jack and Nathan, followed closely by Natasha helping a slower moving Jethro. Hailey dashes down the steps from the watchtower just as the first explosion rips through the night air.

"Quickly, into the tunnel, we don't have much time."

Running down into the escape tunnel Jay turns as Jethro comes through last and seals the entrance with some soil. Not a great defense but at least it will stop any creepers following us down, he thinks. Running to catch up with his friends, he is thrown from side to side as the detonations increase in volume and frequency up above. Sounds like the world is ending, I just hope Jethro and Natasha built this tunnel deep enough or this is going to a very short run to nowhere.

After running for over 300 blocks, Natasha comes to a halt and holds up her hand. Pushing past the others Jay moves to the front of the tunnel and whispers to her.

"What's up, why are we stopping?"

"Trouble. Our tunnel emerges right under that huge monster on the hill. I don't know about you but I would rather not confront it unless I had too."

"Damn. So what are you suggesting?"

"I've been counting the blocks since we left the tower and I think we are just about parallel with that river that runs through the woods behind the village. If we can come up in the woods then jump in a boat we could sail out of here before anyone even knows we are gone."

"Bit chancy don't you think, hoping to find enough boats to just sail out of here?"

"You're not serious are you?"

"What?"

"Holy Notch! Come on Jay, where do you think we are. We build the boats and take them with us."

"Oh, of course. Sorry, I think I must have been hit in the head or something, really thick moment."

"Duh yeah!"

"Right, here's the plan guys," says Natasha turning to the others. "Our original escape route is now compromised so we need a new exit route. I suggest we dig here," she points at the wall on her left, "for 150 blocks, which will bring us up in that little wood behind the village. Once we come up there will be a fast flowing river, we jump in our boats and sail the heck out of here."

"Uh, but we don't have any boats?" chirps in Jack.

Looking at Jay, Natasha replies. "Guess it runs in the family." Looking back at Jack Natasha answers. "Jay and Jethro are going to make some boats while we dig the tunnel. Jethro, you have everything you need?"

Reaching into his inventory Jethro looks up and replies. "I've got everything apart from a crafting table."

Reaching into her inventory, Natasha pulls out her crafting table and hands it to Jethro. "Right, six boats as fast as possible." Turning, she pulls two stone pickaxes from her inventory and hands one to Nathan. "Come on kid, you're digging with me, I'll dig the top block, you dig the bottom. Jack, follow on behind and place torches every 20 blocks, let's move."

Like a well-oiled machine, Natasha and Nathan start digging into the tunnel wall and are soon moving towards the river. Immediately, Jethro and

Jack set to work making boats. On his crafting table Jethro places a block of wood, turning it into planks which he quickly arranges three on the bottom and one on either side. Amazingly, when he lifts this from the table he is holding a small canoe like boat in his hands. A gasp from behind alerts him that Hailey is still with them.

"It never ceases to amaze me how you do that," she smiles.

"I know, cool right?"

"Way cool."

Smiling, Jethro bends back to the table, quickly making five other boats. Jay has his own crafting table and is working furiously when Hailey moves over to him."

"What you making Jay?"

"Just one second more. Right, here, it's not much but it will help." Handing Hailey a leather breastplate and leggings he looks sheepishly at the floor. "Like I said, it's not much but should stop an arrow if it has too."

Hugging and kissing him on the cheek, Hailey grabs the armor and throws it on over her clothes. "Thank you Jay. That's the nicest thing anyone has every done for me in minecraft."

Blushing, and looking bashful, Jay replies, "You're welcome Hailey."

Chuckling in the background Jethro smiles. Young love, now isn't that sweet.

Putting his crafting table back in his inventory, Jethro turns to Jay. "You good the go?"

"Yeah, let's do it." Grabbing 3 boats each, they put them into their inventories, receiving a shocked gasp from Hailey.

"What's wrong?"

"Nothing, sorry. It's that you both just picked up three boats each and shoved then inside yourselves. It's just so freaky weird."

Looking at each other, they both shrug.

"Suppose it is but it's starting to just seem normal to us. Let's move. I don't know how much time we have before they discover we're not dead."

Running down the lighted corridor, Jay grabs the torches as he passes and puts them back into his inventory. Never know when they might come in handy again.

★★★★★

"Right guys, you all set?" asks Natasha, standing at the end of the tunnel. "Good, I'll go up first and take a quick look around. If I'm right, the river should be just a few blocks on our left. When I give the signal, all come up, get in your boat quietly, and head down stream. All good?"

Everyone nods in agreement.

"Good, Jethro, pass out the boats, everyone take your own so we can move quickly."

"Uh, sorry to be a pain Natasha, but I can't carry mine."

"No worries Hailey, I'll carry yours for you," replies Jay.

"Right, that's sorted, let's move."

Digging as quietly as she can, Natasha breaks a block above her and moon light floods the tunnel. Gingerly she pokes her head out and looks around. Dropping back into the tunnel, she whispers all clear and continues to break an exit from the tunnel. On her signal, they all grab their boats, silently exit the tunnel, and creep to the waters edge. Through the trees fires burn in the distance and small explosions continue to detonate in what remains of the village. As the last person exits the tunnel, Natasha fills in the entrance with soil and hides their escape route. Quickly boarding their boats, they are swiftly swept down stream, away from the night's terrible destruction.

★★★★★

Chapter 6

New Strategies

"Slow down boss, I need to take a break, my leg's killing me."

"If you don't shut up and keep moving I'll kill you myself. Now be quiet."

Suitably chastised Warlord continues to trudge along behind the others. He never imagined how painful an arrow wound could be. Normally, when he played, he killed everything in his path, mobs, players whatever, it made no difference to him. Now he was starting to question whether he would be able to use this tactic here as getting hurt really, well, hurt! He was getting pretty fed up with PowerGlide too. After all, they had all been invited here because they were great minecraft players, but here he was acting like the sidekick in some bad superhero movie. Ordered around, insulted, and treated like an idiot. Making up his mind, he gradually dropped behind the others until they were out of sight then took off into the forest, determined to make a go of it on his own. Finding a small clearing, he digs a 2x2x2 hole and jumps in. Turning, he covers the roof with soil, lights a torch and settles in for the night, planning to wait out the rest of the night and assess his new situation in the morning.

*****

Barreling along at a good rate of knots Jethro removes a coil of rope from his inventory and ties it to his boat. Catching Natasha's eye, he throws her the coil, "tie the boats together so we don't get separated," he shouts above the noise of the rushing water.

"Good idea Jethro." Tying her boat, she attracts Nathan's eye and throws the rope to him who repeats the process until all six boats are tied together.

"So, what now Hailey, do you know where this river goes?" asks Jethro.

"Sorry, I've no idea. I haven't ventured too far from the village since I've been here and the villagers never go very far. A few players came from this direction a few years ago but they were more interested in killing than talking."

"Yeah, I get that. Most players seem to take delight in killing everything, mobs, villagers, other players. Makes no difference to them, that's why I turned to creative, much more peaceful."

Strangely, as the river widens it starts to pick up speed and the scenery suddenly starts to change from lightly wooded plains to densely forested jungle. Almost immediately, the temperature soars and the air becomes thick and wet with moisture.

"Well I guess we just entered a new biome, jungle if I'm not mistaken," announces Jethro to the group.

"You think? What gave it away?" replies Natasha sarcastically to numerous giggles.

"The increase in temperature and humidity is indicative of a jungle biome plus of course the jungle foliage as exampled by ...."

"Jethro, we know, ok. She was being sarcastic," interrupts Jay.

"Oh, sorry. I really did not realize. My bad, I think that's the right expression, is it not?"

"Yeah J-Dog, it's cool," replies Nate.

"J-Dog, I quite like that, thank you Nathan. I feel quite hip and cool."

"Hip and cool? man Jethro, you really need to tell us what century you're from," laughs Nate.

"Ok guys, keep it down, we don't know what's around the next bend but we better expect the worst."

Settling down, the six companions nervously sit in their boats as they rapidly approach the river bend. Expecting trouble, they remove swords, spears, and bows from their inventories and prepare for battle.

As they round the bend, they confront a gigantic monster, but not the one that they were expecting. Ahead of them, the river begins to fall away, until it crashes over a precipice as a raging waterfall.

"Quick Hailey, we need a safety line."

Looking at where Jethro is pointing she immediately grabs the end of the rope, ties it to an arrow, and fires it into a huge tree growing on the riverbank. Immediately the line draws taught and the boats swing around, dangling off the line.

"Good shot girl, way to go" shouts Natasha. "Can you climb up the line?"

"I don't know, but I'll give it a try."

Grabbing the line, she pulls herself along, dangling underneath until she reaches the bank. Dropping to the floor, she calls out for the next person. One by one, they pull themselves along the line until just Natasha and Jethro are left in the boats.

"Ok Jethro, you're up next."

"No, after you young lady. I feel my rather corpulent figure may have a detrimental effect on the rope."

"Not a chance Jethro, you think I'm leaving you here on your own? Now get out before I throw you out."

Grimacing, Jethro grabs the rope and starts to pull himself along the line. All is going well until a large log comes barreling around the corner and slams into the leading boat. Immediately the line snaps, throwing Jethro into the water and sending Natasha swirling away towards the jaws of the mighty waterfall.

★ ★ ★ ★ ★

Advancing cautiously into the clearing in the woods, PowerGlide sniffs the air. Smells like zombies, he thinks, drawing his sword and moving towards the small wooden house at the far side. As he draws closer, he spots dark shadows moving at the tree line. "Zombies at 3 o'clock, defensive positions." Immediately they each turn their backs into the centre and form a circle. "Where the hell is Warlord?" barks PowerGlide.

"No idea boss," replies Munster. "Now that I think of it I haven't heard him moaning for quite a while."

"Well, thinking has never been your strong point, has it?" PowerGlide snaps back.

"Get stuffed Glide. It's not my fault he's gone," he snarls.

"Yeah? But it is your fault that you never noticed. Now get back there and find him."

"No way, there are zombies everywhere."

"We'll take care of the zombies, you find Warlord and get back here asap. Now move it!"

Running out of the clearing, back in the direction they had just travelled, Munster cannot help but wonder why he is taking orders from PowerGlide, it is supposed to be a competition after all.

"Right Mad, just you and me. Think you can handle a few zombies?"

"No probs Glide, slice em' and dice em'."

"Good man, because here they come."

Shuffling into the clearing, twenty plus zombies advance on their position.

"Uh boss, that's a lot of zombies. How do you want to play this?"

"Hold your position, face forward, I've got your back. Come on man, look ahead, they're almost on us."

As the zombies shuffle into range, PowerMad steps forward and cleaves the heads off the first two with a single swing. "Hey boss, you see that, they're having a two for one sale on zombie heads. Boss, you ok boss?"

Looking over his shoulder he see's PowerGlide disappearing into the woods and another dozen zombies advancing on his position from behind.

"You bastard! Get your stinking ass back here you dirty little..." but he does not get to finish his tirade as three zombies grab hold of him and pull him to the floor.

"Get your stinking, rotten flesh off me." Punching one zombie in the face, he raises his leg and kicks another as it tries to bite his ankle. With no time to spare he swings his sword and slices the heads from two of the zombies and rolls to the side as three more arrive and try to hold him down.

"You need to be faster than that, meat head," he bellows, swinging his sword and kicking out at any zombie that is unfortunate enough to come into his path. Fighting his way towards the edge of the clearing, leaving thirty plus dead zombies in his wake he stumbles over a fallen log and drops to his knees. Immediately the zombies sense a change in their fortune's and rush forward. Shuffling backwards on his knees, PowerMad continues to delivery deadly blow after deadly blow. Arms and legs are hewn from bodies, and the stench of rotting flesh is almost overpowering. Backing into, what he thinks is a tree, he prepares to stand as he feels the razor sharp bite of a zombie sinking its teeth into his neck.

"Nooooo," he screams, grabbing the zombie by its neck and throwing it over his shoulder at the advancing hoard. Feeling his life point's plummet, he looks wildly about him for options. Seeing the small cabin, with its door wide open, he pushes himself to his feet and, screaming a war cry, runs straight for it. Knocking zombies aside as he dashes for the safety of the cabin his pace starts to slow, and zombie hands reach out for him. As he nears the front door, he has four zombies clinging to him, trying to drag him down. Stumbling forward, he senses his life points falling rapidly and cannot believe that he is going to loose to a zombie. Screaming his defiant war cry, he throws off the zombies hands and turns to face his aggressors. "Come on you meat heads, come and get it ...arrggh....arrggh."

The zombies shuffle to a halt and stand defeated in front of him. They no longer fear or loath him, it is as if he no longer exists to them. Slowly they lose interest and shuffle off in different directions. When PowerMad is finally alone he looks around, gives out a huge moan, and shuffles off after his fellow zombies.

*****

Hanging on the rope, Jethro is tossed like a rag doll in the current. With his strength fading he looks towards the bank where Jack, Jay, Hailey and Nathan pulling on the rope.

"Hold on Jethro, just a little longer," shouts Jay over the thunderous sound of rushing water. After minutes of strenuous rope pulling, they finally manage to heave Jethro from the water and he drops, exhausted on the riverbank.

"Thank you," splutters Jethro. "I thought I was done for that time." Looking about he asks. "Where's Natasha?"

"Sorry Jethro. When the line broke, Natasha was still in the front boat and they all went over the waterfall."

"What? Nooooo. I told her I was too heavy and she should have gone first. This is all my fault."

"It's not your fault Jethro," replies Hailey, bending down and comforting him. "A huge log came around the river bend and slammed into the boats, that's what snapped the line."

"Even so, if Natasha had gone first then she would still be alive."

"Uh guys. Has anyone heard an announcement?" asks Nate.

"What?"

"Has anyone heard an announcement? When someone dies, that announcer dude tells everyone who is dead. Now I haven't heard anything, so maybe Natasha is still alive."

"My lord, he's right," smiles Jethro heaving himself from the riverbank. "Come on everyone, we have to help her."

Rushing along the edge of the river as the sun is starting to rise they fail to notice the dozens of eyes watching them from the jungle foliage.

★ ★ ★ ★ ★

Sprinting through the wood, PowerGlide quickly catches up with Munster.

"Come on man, we need to get moving," he shouts as he sprints past him and disappears around the corner.

Chasing after PowerGlide, Munster runs along side him and asks, "where's Mad? what happened?"

"Too many zombies. They came from everywhere. We got separated in the clearing, and the last I saw, they were all over PowerMad. There is no way he could have survived. We need to put some distance between us and them before morning."

"Crap, it's Warlord's fault. If we were all together we would have been alright."

"Couldn't agree more. Warlord is certainly the cause of all our problems. We need to think very carefully what to do with him when we catch up with him."

"I know what I'm going to do to that dirty little coward when I catch up with him."

Smiling to himself, PowerGlide thinks, I love it when a plan comes together. Before long, I will be the last player, and crowned Master of Minecraft.

✱ ✱ ✱ ✱ ✱

Chapter 7

And Another One Bites The Dust

Opening his eyes, Notch looks around his surroundings. He appears to be in a 6 x 4 granite cell with iron bars at the front. Two flaming torches light the cell.

"Hello Notch, I hope you are feeling ok after your trip here?"

"Where am I and who are you?"

"You are home and I think you know who I am," he replies, stepping forward into the light.

"Herobrine?"

Standing before him is a blocky character with shinning yellow eyes.

"Of course. I'm so happy that we are finally together Notch."

"What the heck is happening?"

"The future!"

"What? Cut the crap, where am I, and what the hell is going on?"

"You are in the world of our making. You have now taken your rightful place in the world of Minecraft."

"What? But, that is not possible, what sort of joke is this? Who put you up to this?"

"Why, you did Notch. You agreed to come with me and take up your rightful place with me."

"I most certainly did not."

"Yes Notch, you did. No one can enter minecraft unless they agree to come. I asked you if you were ready, and you said yes."

"But, but, but that's not what I meant."

"Whatever, you are here, as you should be. Now we can begin."

"Begin what?"

"Why, the merge, of course."

"What's the merge?"

"Come now Notch, you designed Minecraft. This is all your conception. You designed the merge."

"No, it can't be. Please tell me it's not what I think it is."

"Of course it is Notch. Such genius. Pure and beautiful in its simplicity and it's all down to you. Now are you ready to begin?"

"Noooo."

Even as his scream fades, darkness clouds his vision and he feels himself falling. His last view is of the iron bars opening and Herobrine advancing into the cell.

★ ★ ★ ★ ★

As they reach the edge of the waterfall, the immensity of the situation hits them. Standing on the precipice, they look out at the jungle vista, maybe 150 blocks below them.

"Wow! I've never seen a waterfall this huge before. Look at the jungle, we can see for thousands of blocks."

"Yes, yes Jay, but we need to get down to Natasha. How much rope do you have?"

"Uh, just a few pieces of string, sorry."

"Ok, does anyone else have any rope?" Looking at each player, they all shake their heads in reply.

"Damn and blast it. Right, think Jethro, think. Ok, we will build a staircase down the rock face. Ok everyone, get your pickaxes out, it's time to dig." Removing his own pickaxe, he furiously starts digging at the edge of the cliff face but only gets three blocks deep before hitting granite. "Damn and blast it to damnation." Moving sideways, he digs another block before hitting more granite. Turning again, he starts to dig when a shout from Jay stops him.

"Not that way Jethro. That get's you fresh air."

Looking back at Jay, Jethro drops his axe and slumps to the ground. "This whole cliff face is granite. There's no way we can dig through it with these stone pickaxes."

"I get the feeling that's the idea. No doubt there is a way down but we are going to have to follow the path, and whatever Herobrine has in store for us."

"Arrgghh! I'm sorry Natasha," screams Jethro.

"Give yourself a break man. It is not your fault and anyway, she is still alive. She is tough as nails Jethro. Remember, she was invited here, just like us, because she is a great player, so quit worrying. Now let's get out of here before anything else happens."

"Uh Jay, I wish you hadn't said that," stammers Jack.

Looking back, Jack is pointing at the Jungle. Turning to look where he is pointing he sees hundreds of eyes peering at him from the shadows.

✷ ✷ ✷ ✷ ✷

Sensing a change in the atmosphere, Warlord digs a block of soil from over his head and breathes a sigh of relief as the first rays of daylight fill the opening. He pulls himself from his small shelter and surveys his surroundings. At the edge of the clearing, dark shapes move in the shadows. Their moaning increases as they see him rise up out of the ground.

Son of a bitch. They knew I was here. If it were not for the sun, I would have come up right in the middle of them. Moving cautiously away from the hoard they follow, in the shadows, and he is soon walking in circles, with the hoard of zombies following in the tree line. Suddenly a wail of agony from behind makes him spin. Watching, a zombie rushes from the woods and suddenly bursts into flames. Even as it burns it still advances on him and he finds himself drawing his sword, ready to defend himself. With only a few blocks remaining between him and the flaming zombie, it trips and flails on the floor until it disappears leaving behind some floating cobblestone, a sword, pickaxe, and four gold bars.

What the heck? Zombies do not carry stuff.

BOOM. The canon sound explodes in the air and then the thunderous voice announces...

The forth competitor has been eliminated. PowerMad has not proven worthy. Eight competitors remain. Continue the tournament.

Ah crap, PowerMad. How the hell did you let a zombie get you? Bending down he collects the last possessions of his friend and looks around him again. Mind you, these zombies are very persistent.

✶ ✶ ✶ ✶ ✶

As the canon sounds, Jethro throws his hands over his head and falls to his knees. Screaming at the sky, he does not hear the announcement of PowerMad's demise. Running over to his friend, Nate pries Jethro's hands from his ears and shakes him until he looks into his eyes.

"Jethro, Jethro. It's not Natasha, she's still ok."

Looking into his eyes, Jethro asks pleadingly, "What? It's not Natasha, she's still ok?"

"Yes Jethro, PowerMad just bought the farm, but Natasha is still ok, at least for now."

"Oh thank the lord." Grabbing Nate, he encloses him in a huge bear hug. Laughing and literally jumping with joy, Jethro spins around and around.

"Guys, cool it, we still have company."

Looking over at Jay, Jethro immediately sobers up and puts Nate down.

"So what do you think it is Jay?"

"I don't know Jack, just keep still and whatever it is won't come out in daylight."

"Yeah right, just like creepers don't come out in daylight either."

"Oh snap, that's it Jay, you still got that string?"

"Yeah."

"Good, very slowly get your crafting table out and make me a fishing rod."

"What! We don't have time for this Hailey."

"Shut up Jay, I know what I'm doing. Come on, don't just stand there."

Looking at her, Jay shrugs and pulls his crafting table from his inventory. Reaching back inside, he pulls out two lengths of string and combines them with three poles on the crafting table. Handing the fishing rod to Hailey, he remarks, "You better know what you're doing, because whatever they are in the trees they are getting restless."

"Trust me Jay, this is the best thing that has happened, since we met."

Moving slowly, keeping her eyes on the forest, Hailey edges towards the river, and drops the fishing line in the water. Almost immediately, she has a bite and pulls a fish out on the end of her line.

"Ok, everyone stay very still and don't make any noise," she says, dropping the fishing rod and edging closer to the tree line and whatever it contains. As she comes close to the trees a low growl emanates from straight in front of her. Swallowing her fear, she holds out the fish and continues towards the trees.

"Oh clever girl," whispers Jethro.

Turning, Nate asks, "why J, what's she up to?"

"Just watch Nathan, this should be interesting."

Turning back to watch Hailey, Nate neatly jumps out of his skin when a huge, spotted cat moves out of the jungle straight towards Hailey. Just as he is about to shout a warning, a hand clamps over his mouth and Jethro whispers into his ear. "Steady now Nathan, its ok, just watch."

As the giant cat moves towards Hailey she gives a little purring noise and quietly says, "here kitty, come on, you know you want the fish."

Shaking the fish right in front of the cat's face, it sniffs the offering, then gently takes it from her hand and sits down to eat it. Almost immediately, its appearance starts to change, with the spots merging into one another and before long, it looks just like a normal cat, except it is huge. Turning to her audience, Hailey smiles, and asks, "So, who wants their own tamed Ocelot?"

Moving forward slowly to the river, Jay picks up the rod and casts into the fast flowing water. He too is rewarded with a bite and pulls a fish from the water. Holding it up he stage whispers to Jethro, "J-Dog, you're up man, go get yourself an Ocelot."

Moving cautiously towards Jay, who continues fishing, Jethro collects the fish and heads over to where Hailey is playing with her cat. Holding out the fish, he edges towards the forest and is greeted by a loud, deep growl.

"Nice kitty, come on kitty. I've got a lovely fish for you."

The Ocelot that moves out of the shadows is even larger than the first and stands almost as tall a Jethro. Gulping, Jethro waves the fish, and the ocelot moves to within reach, takes the fish and sits down to eat it's prize. As with Hailey, the ocelot immediately changes color to resemble a huge domestic cat.

"Nate, Jack, come on, get a fish," whispers Jay, holding up two wiggling fish.

They both take the fish and perform the same slow and steady dance and before long, they are both sat stroking a huge cat. When Jay catches a fish for himself, he also performs the ocelot dance and is soon a proud cat owner. Once everyone has a cat the other ocelots in the forest lose interest and disappear back to where they came from.

"So Hailey, you want to explain to me why we all just adopted a huge cat? Don't get me wrong, he's really nice," he stammers as the ocelot looks up and places his huge nose right in Nathan's face, "will they protect us, is that the idea?"

"Yes and no Nate, ocelots are peaceful creatures and never attack anything."

"Then why bother, I know I'm new here but everyone else must know that they are useless."

To this comment, he receives a loud, deep growl from all the ocelots.

"No Nate, ocelots are not useless, it is true that they are peaceful and never attack but they have one special skill, creepers are terrified of them and never attack when there are ocelots around."

"Seriously?"

"Yes Nate, seriously. These beauties could be our life savers, literally."

Grabbing his ocelot around the neck, Nathan gives it a huge hug and kisses it on its mussel.

Laughing, the others also hug their ocelots and silently give thanks that at least the creepers will not be a problem anymore.

★ ★ ★ ★ ★

Moving around the clearing, Warlord continues to test the zombie's perimeter. As he moves to the far side of the clearing the zombies move with him, but as the sun rises they are forced further and further back into the trees shadows, so slowing their response time. After about twenty minutes, Warlord realizes that the zombies are starting to move away. No longer able to pursue him, due to the devastating rays of sunlight that are falling through the foliage. Taking advantage of this opportunity, he moves to one side of the clearing, waiting for all the zombies to follow him, and then sprints straight across the clearing and into the trees. Keeping at a sprint it is not long before all signs of zombies are far behind him and he slows to a steady jog. Trying to stay in sunlight, wherever possible, after all this is minecraft, he makes his way east, hoping to find something that will give him some idea as to what he should do next.

★ ★ ★ ★ ★

Sitting in a tree, looking over a small clearing, Munster turns to PowerGlide. "So boss. What do you think?"

"Looks promising, makes sense for Warlord to dig himself in and wait out the darkness. Do you still have your bow?"

"Sure boss, not so many arrows though."

"Ok, I'm going to take a look at that pit, see if there is any evidence that Warlord was here. You keep an eye on those zombies. If they even look like they are going to move, put them down."

"No problem boss, but you're safe in the sunlight, you know that."

"Safe now, but what happens when all the rules change again?"

"Then I put the zombies down for you. So, are you going or what?"

Looking hard at Munster, PowerGlide jumps from the tree and moves cautiously into the clearing. As he approaches the pit, he can see a few small cubes of cobblestone floating above the ground. So, looks like a player died here, must have been PowerMad. I sure hope he never got a chance to speak to Warlord before he bought it or my job just got a hell of a lot harder. Turning to Munster, he waves him over.

"What's the story boss?"

"Look here, cobblestone, looks like Warlord spent the night here and cleaned out his inventory before he left."

"Yeah, makes sense. So where did he go?"

"Trail leads that way." Walking to the tree line, they see a clear trail between the trees. "Looks like he had a lot of company following him when he left."

"Sure does boss." Bending, Munster examines the trail. "Looks like a couple of hundred zombies and something else."

"Oh, what?"

"No idea boss, I've never seen anything like it before. So, what now?"

"Hm, I think we leave our unfaithful friend to play with his new acquaintances. No point getting caught up in his zombie squabble now, is there."

"Guess not boss, but I sure would like to get even with him."

"And rest assured, if we ever meet up with Warlord again, we will exact our vengeance. Now come on, day light's burning and we have other game to hunt."

★ ★ ★ ★ ★

Chapter 8
New Beginnings

"So, how are we going to make these Ocelots come with us?" asks Nathan, getting up from the ground.

"You don't make an ocelot do anything," replies Hailey.

"Exactly! They're huge, we can't exactly tie a rope around their necks and drag them."

"You don't have to Nate, just walk over there and see what happens," Hailey replies pointing to a small rock formation, maybe 30 blocks away.

Following her lead, Nate walks over the the outcrop and is amazed that the ocelot tags along with him.

"Cool, does this mean that it will follow me everywhere?"

"Yes Nate, you just tamed your first ocelot. It will now follow you, wherever you go. The only things that it is afraid of are wolves."

"Way cool, it's like having a pet tiger."

"Better I'd say, you won't wake up in the morning with an ocelot chewing on your leg."

"Um, this is all very interesting, and thank you Hailey for the ocelots, but maybe now we can get back to finding Natasha?"

"Yes, of course Jethro, so has anyone any ideas?"

"I think the only thing we can do is follow the cliff face and see where it leads us, no doubt there will be some way down," replies Jack.

"Sounds like a plan, all agreed?"

"Hang on a second, this is minecraft, yeah, and in minecraft, you can fall from as high as you like as long as you land in water. So, I know it's scary, but maybe we should just go over the waterfall, like Natasha."

"Are you joking? that could kill us."

"But it didn't kill Natasha, Jack."

"Says who?"

"Says the game. No announcement means no death."

"Sorry to interrupt your little squabble boys, but just in case you have not noticed, I'm human."

As all eyes turn to Hailey, they nod their understanding.

"Be that as it is, I think Jay has made a very valid point, Natasha is my friend and we swore to stick together. I think you guys should follow the cliff face and find a way down, I'll go over the waterfall and find Natasha, then we can meet up somewhere down there," points Jethro.

"Wow guys, we can't start splitting up, haven't any of you ever seen a horror movie. The moment someone says, 'let's split up it's the start of the killing."

"I know Jack, but we need to decide now, before it starts getting dark."

"Jethro, we need to stick together."

"Yes Jack, that would be best, but we also need to find Natasha, and Hailey can not jump over that waterfall and survive. So, I have decided. I am going to find Natasha, the only question left is where do we meet?" asks Jethro, looking out over the vast jungle below him.

"Not so fast Jethro, I'll come with you."

All eyes turn to Nate.

"What? we can't let him go on his own."

"Are you sure Nate?"

"Yeah I'm sure Jay. I like Natasha and if I can help her, I will. Look, over to the left, there is a stone building sticking up through the trees. Let us meet there tomorrow, at midday."

Looking out into the jungle where Nathan is pointing, Jay replies. "That's a temple Nate, could be mobs in there."

"Yes indeed, but it is a landmark in this almost uniform jungle. Right, Nathan, if you are sure that you wish to accompany me, then I would be delighted to have you along. Everyone else, good luck, and we will see you at the temple tomorrow."

Picking up his meager belongings, Jethro removes his crafting table from his inventory. Placing boards on the crafting table, he quickly makes a couple of new boats.

"Right Nathan, if you're coming, then we need to get going."

Turning to the group, Jethro holds out his hand to Jay, "It's been a pleasure Jay, it fact, it's been a pleasure to meet all of you." Turning away quickly, Jethro jumps into his boat and pushes it into the water. To his surprise, his ocelot jumps in with him, almost sinking his boat. Still very new to the ocelot owning experience, he is very unnerved having a 200 Ilb cat snuggled up so close.

"Right, see you guys tomorrow, don't be late," jokes Nate, jumping into his boat. As with Jethro, his ocelot jumps in beside him. "Right Jethro, shall we get this carnival on the road?"

"Yes indeed Nathan, and good luck."

Pushing off from the bank, the boats rapidly gain speed and shoot towards the waterfall edge.

Standing on the bank, the others watch as their friends disappear over the edge of the falls, and the last thing they hear is Nate shouting. "To infinity and beyond!"

✻ ✻ ✻ ✻ ✻

Moving at a fast jog, without encountering any problems, Warlord has covered thousands of blocks over the last couple of hours. The terrain has gradually been changing from wooden plains to more thickly forested. In fact, in the last few blocks, it has turned hot and humid and the foliage has become almost jungle like. At this thought, he stops in his tracks and takes a careful look around. Yep, change of biome, he thinks, looks like I am into a jungle biome now, this is going to slow me down. Removing his sword, he uses it as a machete to help cut a way through the ever-thickening vegetation. Trying to stay in the less heavily forested sections he continues to move east, he is not really sure why, but he needs to head somewhere. Checking behind him he sees he has left a very obvious trail. Man, I hope I lost those zombies before I entered this jungle or I am going to be dead easy to find. Stopping at a large tree, he decides to climb it and take a survey of the surrounding area. Reaching the top, after a few hairy moments, he pushes his head through the canopy and gasps. Jungle stretches as far as the eye can see. It is a vast field of green, only broken by a wide blue river. Yes, that is where I need to go. Taking a bearing on the river, he climbs down and heads in that direction.

✻ ✻ ✻ ✻ ✻

"So what's the plan boss?" asks Munster as he jogs along the edge of the tree line.

"Find the other group of players, and finish them off. I can't believe they got away from all those creepers and zombies."

"I know, I thought for sure that they were goners."

"Right, but they must have found a way out, so let's head back to the village, and see what we can see."

"Cool boss, but I sure don't want to be around come nightfall. If we're caught out in the open, with that many creepers, then we're done for."

"You're not wrong there Munster. Right, double time, let's get to the village with a little daylight to spare."

Sprinting along the tree line, they spy the village after about twenty minutes.

"Ok Munster, slow down, let us approach with a little caution. Those creepers were out in the daytime yesterday, let's not walk straight in on them."

Moving stealthily along the edge of the tree line, the village, or what is left of it, slowly comes into view.

"WTF! It's gone," exclaims Munster.

Where the village had once stood is now a battlefield of craters. The surrounding wall is still pretty much intact, but everything inside is now destroyed.

"There must have been a hell of an explosion to create that much damage."

"Yeah, or lots or small ones," replies PowerGlide pointing at the hundreds of small craters that join together, all through the village. "Looks like they made a last stand here, but how did they manage to get away?"

"Maybe they flew?" jokes Munster.

"Well, it's possible in creative mode but I've never heard of it in survival before."

"Yeah, but this is not exactly a normal game of minecraft, is it?"

"Guess you're right, but let's take a look around for other options first."

Spreading out they start to search the area, looking for any sign that the other players passed through.

"Hey boss, over here."

"What did you find Munster?

"Look, a tunnel." Pointing at the bottom of a particularly large crater, where the bottom had blown out the roof of a tunnel below.

"Nice work. Seems our friends were more prepared than I gave them credit for. Let's take a little lookey see where this leads, shall we?"

Jumping into the tunnel, they both light a torch and draw their swords.

"Ok boss, that way slants up so I bet you would find they tunnel entrance if you followed it, so I guess we go this way."

Jogging along the tunnel, stopping only to place torches they soon arrive at the intersection.

"So, which way boss?"

"Judging the direction, and the straightness of the tunnel I'd say that this way," pointing straight ahead, "goes to that small hill behind the village. Now last night, that giant black monster was stood on top of the hill, so I'm guessing that's why they stopped and dug this other tunnel."

"Yeah, makes sense. So, where does this tunnel go?"

"No idea, so why don't we go and find out?"

Jogging down the intersection, they arrive at a dead end with steps rising to the ceiling.

"Clever buggers, they covered their exit point after they left so the mobs would not know which way they went."

"Yeah, but do you think it worked?"

Looking around the tunnel, PowerGlide replies. "Yeah, looks like it, if a thousand creepers had been through here there would be signs, and the tunnel is still sealed. I've never heard of a creeper placing blocks before, have you?"

"Nah, you're right boss. So what now?"

"Guess we follow the trail," he replies smiling and removing a stone pickaxe from his inventory. Moving up the stairs he breaks the two blocks sealing the tunnel and daylight flows in. "Come on Munster, we have some players to catch up with."

"Hold on one minute boss, be right there." Dashing back down the tunnel, Munster removes his pickaxe and starts workings at the walls. After breaking 15 blocks, he dashes back up the exit and up the stairs into daylight.

"What took you so long?"

"Just spotted some iron ore, so grabbed it before we moved on."

"Good work, how much you got now?"

Looking in his inventory, Munster replies. "I've got 30 iron ores and 3 iron ingots, how about you?"

"I've got 12 iron ingots and 8 iron ores, that's enough for two sets of amour. Let's take five and re-equip ourselves before we move on. You make the ingots, I'll do the armor."

"Cool boss."

Removing his forge from his inventory, Munster loads it up with his, and PowerGlide's iron ore, then stokes the furnace with wood chunks. Before too long, iron ingots start falling out of the furnace, which he hands to PowerGlide, who arranges them on his crafting table to construct a suit of iron armor. Laying three ingots across the middle then one at either end he constructs a helmet, three across the top then two at either end, he has some leggings. Placing eight ingots on his table with one missing at the top centre builds a chest plate, then for the final time he places two sets of two ingots on the table and makes some boots. With a complete set of iron armor, he then repeats the process for Munster. With all the iron ore melted and the armor complete, they climb into their new outfits and admire their work.

"Wow boss, I have done this a million times on minecraft but this is awesome, we just made a suit of armor and it's so light and easy to move in. Feels no different to wearing clothes."

"You're not wrong there Munster, I was worried that we would be slowed down, or cumbersome in the iron armor, that's why I did not bother to make any. Just stuck with my leather chest plate, but this feels really good. Right, let's move out, we need to find where those other players went and set up a defensible position before dark."

Looking around the clearing for any clues as to where the players might have gone they see the river with muddy foot prints at the edge.

"Fools, they go to all the trouble of hiding the tunnel then leave foot prints into the river."

"Yeah boss, but remember you don't have to think of these things in the game, so maybe they just didn't realize?"

"Yeah, but that mistake is going to cost them their lives. The prints show them dragging boats into the river. Looks like were going for a little boat ride."

"Cool!" Removing his crafting table, Munster quickly knocks up a couple of boats and places then on the rivers edge. "Ready to go boss?"

"Right you are Munster, let's go hunting!"

★ ★ ★ ★ ★

Chapter 9

Jungle Time

Turning his head, Jethro smiles at his friends on the riverbank, as his boat drifts towards the falls. Turning to look at Nathan, he is shocked to see a huge grin plastered on his friends face and even more shocked when he punches the air and screams as he disappears over the fall ahead of him.

Waving goodbye to his friends, Nathan turns forward in his small boat, and for the first time the sheer magnitude of the waterfall grips him. Instead of fear, he feels excited and alive. Smiling with anticipation as his boat picks up speed, he is swiftly pulled towards the precipice. As the boat reaches the edge he punches the air and on impulse screams, at the top of his lungs.

"To infinity and beyond!"

As the boat starts its plunge into the mist created by the crashing water, Nathan cannot help but compare it to his favorite ride at Disney land, the log flume, although this is the biggest log flume ever invented, and surely, no one sane would ever ride it. Falling through the mist, into a torrent of millions of gallons of water, his stomach rises into his mouth, his heart rate increases, and a feeling of weightlessness almost lifts him from the boat. Gripping the sides and pushing back against his ocelot, trying to keep them both in, they plummet towards the river below. 150 blocks worth of rushing, bubbling water shoots by, and as Nathan reaches the bottom, his boat hits the water at what feels like a thousand miles an hour. Incredibly, instead of shattering, the boat plunges below the surface, travels for 20 plus blocks underwater then surfaces in a spray of foam, rising 20 blocks into the air before once again slamming down onto the river surface.

"Yeeha! That was awesome," he screams, turning to make sure his ocelot is still with him. Clinging to the boat, with extended nails, the ocelot is still there, but not looking quite as thrilled as Nathan looks. "Yes, Flumey my buddy, we made. Cool, Flumey, that's your name." Smiling, he gives him a huge hug and turns in alarm as a terrified scream rips the air.

Watching as Jethro plummets down the face of the waterfall, Nathan cannot believe that he had just ridden such a ride. The sheer size alone was enough to numb the senses. Screaming, Jethro is half out of the boat as it hits the water and disappears, only to reappear very close to Nathans boat. Laughing, Nathan quickly paddles over but is shocked to find just a terrified ocelot clinging in the bottom of the boat. Looking all around, Nathan shouts for Jethro, but there is no answer. After a few minutes of panic, paddling as close as he dares to the base of the waterfall, Nathan is starting to fear the worst when a shout from behind him draws his attention.

"And I suppose you enjoyed that?" Standing on the riverbank, looking bedraggled and sickly, is Jethro.

"Jethro! You made it, I was starting to worry."

"Yes, at least I think I'm all here."

"That was the most awesome ride in history. Hey J-Dog, can you believe we rode the waterfall?"

"Yes, quite frankly, the way I am feeling, I can definitely believe that I rode that infernal waterfall."

"Oh come on. That was awesome, you must have enjoyed it."

"Quite the opposite, dear boy. That was the most terrifying thing I have ever had the displeasure to do, in my entire 58 years."

"What?"

"What do you mean what? I said it was the most ..."

"Yeah, yeah. I got that, but you said you were 58!"

"That is correct, and I would like to make it to 59 if at all possible."

"But that's so old Jethro. I thought you were like us."

"Oh, I see what you mean, well rest assured Nathan, that as old as I am, I am still just like you. We were invited here because we are all minecraft addicts, so age really has little bearing on us, just our abilities."

"Speak for yourself Jethro, before I got here I had never even heard of minecraft."

"Right, so really, it is you who is the odd one out, not me. Thank you Nathan, that actually makes me feel a little better."

"Uh, you're welcome, but it's not really what I meant."

"Yes I know, but I think we had better take a little look around before we continue this conversation, don't you?"

"Yeah, you're right. I'll bring your boat over."

As Nathan approach's with Jethro's boat, his ocelot pokes his head from where it had been hiding and gives him a friendly growl.

"Oh I see you made it ok, you big coward. You pushed me out, you're supposed to be my companion, you traitorous back stabber."

Looking suitable sorry, the ocelot jumps from the boat, and gives Jethro a huge lick on his face.

"Get off me you big lump, you, you...." but he cannot finish his sentence as the ocelot playfully pushes him to the floor and continues to lick him. Laughing despite himself, Jethro finally admits defeat and gives him a big hug, "ok, ok, you win. We're still friends."

Laughing, Nathan playfully asks. "So what are you going to call him?"

"I don't think that naming him is such a good idea Nathan. He's here to protect us from creepers, but we have no idea what is ahead for us."

"True, but he is here now and he needs a name. We can't just call him ocelot, or there will be massive confusion with six of them around."

"Quite true, so what do you suggest?"

"Well, I've called my one Flumey, after the log flume ride that we just rode together."

"Yes, very appropriate, so I guess then I will call my one Fawkes, after Guy Fawkes," turning to look at his ocelot with a smile playing at his lips, he continues, "who was also a treacherous beast."

Fawkes looks back at him and gives a playful snarl.

"Good, that's settled, Flumey and Fawkes it is. So what now?"

"Now Nathan, we need to find Natasha."

Getting back into his boat they paddle slowly along the edge of the river, looking for signs that Natasha had survived her fall.

★ ★ ★ ★ ★

Watching their friends disappear over the waterfall is a terrifying experience and Jay cannot help but wonder if he will ever see them again. After waiting anxiously for a few minutes, with no announcements, they decide that their friends must have survived the falls and turn and start their march along the edge of the cliff.

No one speaks for over twenty minutes until Hailey cannot stand the silence any longer.

"Ok, ok, I'm sorry, if it wasn't for me you could have all gone together."

"What?" asks Jay.

"I said that if it wasn't for me you could have all gone together. I never meant to split your group up."

"Of course you didn't Hailey, it's fine. We'll all meet up again tomorrow, at the temple, don't worry about it."

"Really, you mean it?"

"Of course we do, don't we Jack?"

"Yeah, sure, whatever."

"Ok, so what's the plan Jay?"

"Not much we can plan right now, just follow the path, and see if we can find a way down."

"And what happens if there is no way down?"

"Well, I guess we cross that bridge when we come to it."

"Not much of a plan Jay."

"Well, I never said it was. Come on, let's pick the pace up, and see if we can find somewhere before night fall."

Breaking into a jog, the three friends cover a lot of ground before Jay calls them to a halt.

"Hey Jack, look over there, tell me what you see," asks Jay, pointing out over cliff face.

"Jungle Jay, just in case you didn't realize it, there's lots and lots of jungle."

"Yeah smart ass, but what about the jungle?"

Looking at the treetops, Jack studies the terrain until suddenly it dawns on him.

"It's closer, the tops of the trees are way closer."

"Exactly, the drop to the trees can't be more than 50 blocks now, if we keep going at this rate we should be able to find a way down shortly."

"Cool, let's go," replies Jack, dashing off along the path with his ocelot in tow.

Turning to face Hailey, Jay remarks, "kids huh, where do they get their energy?"

Laughing, she turns to face him and replies, "Thanks Jay, for back there, I really appreciate you and Jack staying with me." Reaching up she gives him a kiss on the cheek and dashes off after Jack.

Watching her run off, he reaches up and touches the spot she had just kissed. Smiling, he runs after the others and quickly catches up with Hailey. He reaches out and touches her arm and smiles. She smiles back at him and they run on together for a few more minutes until they catch up with Jack, who is standing at the base of a massive, fallen tree.

"What's up Jack, why have you stopped?"

"Look Jay, if we can move this tree over the edge we could climb down it to the forest, it's only about 50 blocks down."

"Yeah, but how can we move a tree that size?"

"Watch and learn, Jay Lightningbuilder."

Pulling his pickaxe from his inventory, Jack quickly digs around the tree, forming a slope towards the edge of the cliff face. Leaving just one block in place, to prevent the tree from slipping, he turns to face the other two with a huge smile on his face.

"Tada!"

"Tada, my ass. I don't see much difference Jack."

"Oh you of little faith, just watch when I knock out this last block, the tree will slide down the slope and the top end will fall over the edge, so making a nice and convenient ladder for us all to climb down."

"I don't know Jack, how are you going to get out of the way of the tree when it ...."

Jack lifts his axe and breaks the last block, and immediately the tree rushes down the slope towards him. Unable to get out of its path, the best he can do is jump up into its low hanging branches and hold on for dear life. As the tree slides towards the edge of the cliff, Jay jumps forwards, but is knocked to the ground. Shouting to Jack, he runs after the massive tree at it teeters on the edge of the cliff, then plummets over and disappears.

"Noooo, Jack," screams Jay, rushing to the edge of the cliff and peering over the edge. Five blocks below, the tree dangles precariously, supported only by a few stout branches tangled in the cliffside vegetation. Even as he watches, the tree groans and slips another block, wavering dangerously close to plummeting to the bottom.

"Jack, Jack. Where are you?"

"Here Jay," replies Jack, forcing himself through the foliage at the top of the tree.

"Are you ok?"

"Yeah, sorry Jay, I seem to have made a bit of a mess of this."

"No probs bro, let's just get you out of there. Can you work your way along the branch, back to the main trunk?"

"I can't Jay, my leg is stuck in something."

"Right, don't move, I'm coming down to get you."

Immediately the tree slips another couple of blocks and swings out over open air.

"Jay, help, please. I don't want to die."

"Just hold on Jack, I'm coming."

Grabbing his pickaxe, he franticly digs down for 5 blocks before hitting granite. Digging outwards, he knocks an opening in the cliff face and can see Jack just 3 blocks below him and maybe 5 blocks over.

"Hold on Jack, I'm coming to get you, just don't move."

"No Jay, it's too dangerous, if you come out here the tree will fall and we'll both die."

"I have no choice Jack. Can you imagine what mum would say if I came home without you. My life would not be worth living."

"Yeah Jay, I guess mum's the scariest thing around here."

Laughing and glad that Jack was ok he replies, "you're not wrong there Jack, just hold on a second and I'll think of a way to ...."

The tree gives a thunderous crack and slips completely over the edge, plummeting towards the earth. Unable to move, all Jack can do is stare up at his brother as he plummets towards the ground. With an earth shattering crash the tree hits the forest canopy and plunges through to the ground below.

BOOM. The canon sound explodes in the air and then the thunderous voice announces...

The fifth competitor has been eliminated. Jack the Dweeb has not proven worthy. Seven competitors remain. Continue the tournament.

★★★★★

"Over there Jethro, what's that?"

Turning to look in the direction that Nathan is pointing, Jethro strains his eyes trying to make out what he is seeing.

"Can't make it out, what do you see Nathan?"

"I'm not sure, but it's moving around on the bank downstream from us. What do you want to do?"

"Let's proceed with caution. Get your sword ready just in case but be prepared to get the hell out of there if it turns out to be trouble."

Paddling cautiously, they proceed down the river. As they draw closer to the thing on the riverbank, Fawkes gives a low growl.

"Steady boy, let's get a little closer, and see what it is."

At 50 blocks the figure starts charging up the riverbank towards them, screaming, but the words are lost at this distance.

"Careful Nathan, be ready to paddle for all you're worth. We do not know what it is yet and it might be able to swim. Now as we approach... Nathan!"

Paddling like crazy, Nathan pulls ahead of Jethro and shouts happily.

"I know exactly what it is Jethro, it's Natasha, come on."

"Natasha! Of thank goodness."

Paddling hard, Jethro soon catches up to Nathan and they both make it to the riverbank at the same time and find a cross looking Natasha staring at them.

"About time you guys showed up, I wondered how long I would have to wait here before you sent out the search party. I bet you would have been quicker if someone else had gone over the waterfall."

"Sorry Natasha, we tried to get here as soon as possible," stammers Jethro, "but there was no path down and then we ran into the ocelots and it wasn't until ..."

"Shut it Jethro," snaps Natasha. "I don't want an apology from you, what I want is...," rushing forward she grabs hold of Jethro, heaves him from his boat and gives him a huge hug. "Is a huge hug, you wonderful, wonderful man. Thank you, thank you, you too Nate," she smiles, pulling Nate from his boat and hugging him hard. "You guys have no idea what it's like to find you are suddenly on your own here."

As deep, low growls emanate from the boats, Natasha looks over Nathan's shoulder at the two huge ocelots.

"Well now, what do we have here?"

Moving forward slowly towards the ocelots they continue to growl and bare their teeth, with their hackles raised they become quite intimidating.

"Hey guys, cool it, she's with us," shouts Nathan, walking over to his boat and roughly rubbing the back of Flumey's neck, who immediately starts purring. "Flumey, meet Natasha. Natasha, meet Flumey."

Holding out her hand tentatively, she receives a giant lick from Flumey.

"Good, and this one is Fawkes," interjects Jethro.

Receiving another lick from Fawkes, Natasha turns to the lads, "where did you get them, they're so cute."

"Hailey found them in the jungle and showed us how to tame them with fish. It was so cool Natasha, you should have seen it."

"Yes, I'm sure it was, so where are the others?" she asks looking back up the river towards the waterfall in the distance.

"They have gone around by the cliff. Hailey can't come down the waterfall on account of being human and all so we split up to find you."

BOOM. The canon sound explodes in the air and then the thunderous voice announces...

The fifth competitor has been eliminated. Jack the Dweeb has not proven worthy. Seven competitors remain. Continue the tournament.

"Noooo. Not Jack."

"I'm so sorry Nathan. I know he was your real life friend, let's just hope he is now home safe and sound," soothes Natasha, wrapping her arms around him.

"I wonder what happened to the poor boy."

"Not now Jethro, can't you see Nate is upset?"

"Yes, yes, of course. I'm very sorry for your loss Nathan, we both are."

Crying, Nathan looks up at Natasha and asks, "what do you really think happens? is he really dead or will he wake up back at home?"

"I'm not going to lie to you Nate, I really don't know, I hope, really, really hope that we will all end up back home, but nothing like this has ever happened before. Hell, this should not even be happening at all."

"How about you Jethro, what do you think?"

"I think we will all go home at the end of the game Nathan. Anything else is just not worth thinking about. Now, I know we are upset but I really think we need to find somewhere for the night, I can almost feel the sun getting lower as we speak."

"Right, of course, I know just the place, I wasn't just sat on my ass the whole time you were deciding if you were coming for me or not."

"It wasn't like that Natasha, we were always coming to get you it was just..."

"I know Nate, I'm just teasing. Now come with me, once we are secure for the evening we can grieve, until then, there's work to do."

Walking back up the riverbank, Natasha moves into the jungle and disappears from sight.

"Well Nathan, it's time to decide whether you give up or fight on. So, what's it going to be?"

Looking at his friend, he swallows, and gets to his feet.

"Jack would hate me forever if I just gave up, so I guess we fight on, thanks Jethro."

"You're welcome Nathan, now come on, it seems Natasha has something to show us."

Running up the riverbank, with Flumey and Fawkes in tow, they all disappear into the jungle after Natasha.

★★★★★

"Noooo."

Plunging over the waterfall, PowerGlide and Munster scream and hang on to their boats for dear life. Hitting the water at the bottom, they plunge under the surface, only to shoot out 20 blocks further on.

"Arrgghh."

Flying through the air, they slam back down into the water and skim across the surface, eventually coming to rest against the riverbank 80 or 90 blocks further down from the waterfall. Neither of them moves, both still gripping the sides of their boats. First to move is Munster, who peels his fingers from the side of the boat and gives himself a quick pat down. Satisfied that he is in one piece he turns to PowerGlide and asks,

"Hey Glide, you ok boss?"

Receiving no response, he pulls himself from his boat and stumbles over to PowerGlide.

"Hey boss, you ok?" Slapping his face to try to get some response, PowerGlide replies.

"You ever do that again I will kill you."

"Sorry boss, I thought you were catatonic so I slapped you to try and get you to wake up."

"There you go with that again."

"With what boss?"

"Thinking, you see how much trouble you get yourself into ever time you think?"

"Yes boss, sorry, it won't happen again." Yeah, and next time I might just shove a sword down your throat instead of slapping you, he thinks.

"So what now boss?"

"I don't know, this wasn't exactly part of the plan. Give me a second will you."

"Sure boss." Well, well, the all powerful and mighty PowerGlide is suffering after that little pleasure ride. Seems he is not so tough after all.

"Right, first we need to survey the area, check for mobs, players etc. We don't know if anyone else came this way, probably not as you would have to be mad to come over that thing on purpose. Right Munster, you take the left side of the river, I will take the right. Look out for anything interesting."

"Yes boss," he replies, jumping back into his boat and paddling across the river.

BOOM. The canon sound explodes in the air and then the thunderous voice announces...

The fifth competitor has been eliminated. Jack the Dweeb has not proven worthy. Seven competitors remain. Continue the tournament.

Well, well, another one bites the dust. Jack the Dweeb, not someone I have heard of, but one less player is one step closer to winning. Smiling, and humming to himself PowerGlide climbs into his boat and paddles along the right hand side of the river, looking for signs of his next victim.

✹ ✹ ✹ ✹ ✹

Laughing manically, Warlord watches at PowerGlide and Munster slip over the waterfall to their almost certain death. Suddenly dozens of hands grab him roughly and drag him back into the jungle. His laughter turns to a scream as he remembers what was chasing him. Swinging wildly with his sword, he cuts through flesh and bone and severed limbs drop to the floor. For just a moment, the grip that the zombies have on him is released and Warlord takes advantage and throws himself out of the jungle, back into sunlight. Turning to face his attackers, he is surprised when none follows him. Screaming insults at them, he can hardly hear himself over the thunderous roar of the waterfall, when the canon sounds in the air.

"Ha! So long PowerGlide and Munster. So you thought you could out smart me, now look whose dead eh! Not so smart now are you. Ah shut up meat heads, you've lost too so get stuffed!"

Too busy celebrating the demise of his old companions, he does not realize that the announcement was for Jack, not Munster, and PowerGlide. He just assumes that they have died going over the waterfall.

Stumbling up the riverbank to the waterfalls' edge, he stares out over the jungle canopy over 150 blocks below. Better get moving, those zombies will only stay in the jungle until dusk, then I'm in trouble all over again. Running along the cliff edge, with renewed vigor in his stride, Warlord does not see the trees shaking as the zombies try to keep pace with him.

★ ★ ★ ★ ★

Chapter 10

So What Now?

"Jay, come on Jay. Move away from the edge. He's gone, there's nothing you can do."

"No, if I can just get down to him I can save him, I know I can."

"It's too late Jay, the canon has already sounded. I'm afraid he's gone."

"He can't be. He's my brother, he can't be dead."

"Not dead Jay, just gone from the game. He's probably back home now, waiting for you to get back."

"But you don't know that, do you? You said yourself that you don't know if we die here, whether it's real or just in the game."

"I know Jay, but think about it. Hundreds of people have been through here, even since I've been here."

"So?"

"So, have you heard of hundreds of minecraft fans going missing over the last few months?"

"No."

"Exactly, so if they are not going missing then they must get home somehow, ok?"

"Ok, if you really believe that then throw yourself off the cliff and GO HOME!"

"That's not fair Jay." Turning, she runs away from him with tears running down her cheeks.

Realizing what he has done, he pulls himself from the hole and runs after Hailey.

"Wait, Hailey wait. I'm sorry. I didn't mean it."

"I know Jay, but it's hard for me too. You guys are the first people I've really spoken to in years, and now we've lost your brother and it's all my fault."

"What? It's not your fault Hailey, Jack just messed up."

"Yeah, but you still blame me. If you hadn't come this way because of me, then Jack would still be alive."

"No Hailey, I don't blame you, really, I'm just upset."

"Promise?"

"Yes I promise, now come on, let's get down there. I want to make sure that he is really gone. I'll never forgive myself if I don't check and later discover that there was something that could have been done."

"Ok Jay, let's go."

Continuing to follow the trail, they soon find a rough stairs cut into the side of the cliff face.

"Oh Jack, why couldn't you wait just another five minutes. You would still be alive."

Hugging him tight, Hailey whispers into his ear.

"Jay, I know you are suffering and it's not fair to ask this of you, but here goes anyway. I want you to suck it up Jay. You need to get tough, Jack is dead and there is nothing you can do to help him, but you can help yourself. If you wander around here, the way you are, something is going to get you, this is minecraft and it's bloody dangerous. You owe it to Jack to look after yourself. So, what do you say?"

Looking at her with a face like thunder, Hailey thinks she may have pushed Jay too far when he replies through gritted teeth.

"Your right, Jack would hate me if I just gave up after he died. I'm going to win this game for him, and when I do I'm going to find out who set it up and kill them."

"That's the spirit Jay, now let's get out of here. We need to find a place to rest before nightfall."

Moving cautiously down the staircase they descend into the jungle below.

*****

Jogging along the path, Warlord realizes that he is still being followed by the zombies and increases his pace to try to put some distance between them. After sprinting for over thirty minutes he hears voices up ahead and slows his pace, approaching cautiously. Ahead of him he sees Jay and Hailey, just disappearing down a staircase cut into the rock face. Creeping along, he trails them down the stairs and into the jungle.

*****

Paddling slowly along the river, PowerGlide spots two black shapes on the riverbank downstream. Signaling to Munster to approach quietly, they both paddle towards the shapes. As they get closer, they recognize them as boats and scan the tree line for a trap. Not seeing any signs of trouble, they paddle over to the boats, draw their swords, and get out onto the beach.

"So boss, what's the plan?" whispers Munster.

"Scout the beach, quietly. Looks like they headed into the jungle but let's make certain before we walk into a trap."

"Not likely boss, they don't even know that we are on their trail."

"True, but they were being chased by those creepers so they could be expecting trouble. Let's not take the chance, you search the beach above the boats, I'll do below."

After a quick look around, they meet back at the boats.

"Anything boss?"

"No traps. Mind you, there are dozens of large cat prints all over the place that follow them in the forest."

"Yeah, same over here, but it looks like the cats either swam ashore or came with them in the boats."

"Don't be thick Munster. Have you ever heard of a large cat travelling in a boat in minecraft?"

"Uh, no boss, so that means the cats swam ashore and tracked them. Maybe they will do the job for us?"

"If we're lucky, but let's not rely on it. Come on, let's find ourselves some fresh prey," he replies with a wicked smile playing across his face.

✹ ✹ ✹ ✹ ✹

"It's about 150 blocks this way," answers Jay, moving through the forest foliage. Using his sword as a machete, he makes good time and soon arrives at the fallen tree, "Jack, Jack! you here buddy?" he calls out in a stage whisper.

"Shh Jay, let's just take a look around before we make any noise. We haven't scouted the area yet and don't know what's here."

Biting his tongue, trying hard not to call out for his brother, he knows that Hailey is right. Pushing through the heavy foliage, they search the area for any signs of Jack.

"Oh Jay, over here," calls Hailey as quietly as she can.

Running to her side, Jay stops dead in his tracks. Hailey is looking at a group of floating objects, indicating the place that Jack had died.

"I'm so sorry Jay."

Swallowing, he moves forward and collects all of Jacks belongings.

"Right, at least I now know, let's move out, it won't be too long before dark."

Grabbing his arm and stopping him, Hailey looks into his eyes and asks. "Are you ok Jay?"

"It's over Haley. Jack is dead. Like you said, it's time to toughen up."

Walking out from under the giant tree, he continues to cut a path. Looking over his shoulder, he mouths. "The temple is this way, maybe 400 blocks, if we get a move on we can make it before dark."

★ ★ ★ ★ ★

"So, are you going to show us or what?"

"Patience Nate, just a little further."

"Yeah? You said that over 200 blocks back, how far is just a little further anyway?"

"It's about 10 blocks Nate."

"What? But there's nothing here but more jungle."

"Au contraire Nathan my boy. I think Natasha has stumbled onto something quite special here. How in the world did you find it?"

Smiling, she turns to Jethro and pulls up her hair on her forehead showing a nice bruise. "The old fashioned way, I walked straight into it."

"Very clever Natasha, that's using your head," laughs Jethro.

"Oh Jethro, I thought you at least would refrain from bad jokes," she replies slapping her forehead and immediately regretting it.

"Excuse me guys, but what are you talking about?"

"You still can't see it?"

"See what Jethro?"

"Ok Natasha, I guess you had better do the honors."

Smiling, Natasha reaches out and grabs Nathan's hand and smiling, whispers in his ear. "Follow me Nate, step where I step and prepare to be amazed."

Walking carefully into the empty jungle, Nathan suddenly had a feeling a solid object around him, but still he can see nothing but foliage.

"You see it Nate?"

"See what?"

"I think that Nathan needs the same wake up call that you received Natasha."

"Hmm, you could be right, this way Nate, and by the way, I'm sorry."

"Why are you sorry? Ouch." Walking into the side of a huge building, Nathan is a little confused, "where did that wall come from?"

"It was always there Nate, you just had to know what to look for," laughs Jethro.

"And what exactly should I have looked for?"

"Well, you could have looked for a jungle temple that stands over 50 blocks high. That shouldn't have been too hard to see."

"What do you mean, a giant temple that ...." Nathan stops in mid sentence as his field of vision suddenly expands and he is standing in front of a huge, cobblestone temple. "Where the heck did that come from?"

"Is that all you can say Nate, look about. Isn't it wonderful?"

Stepping back from the wall, Nathan surveys the area and realizes that he is looking at a huge temple rising through the trees into the sky.

"Wow guys, how come I couldn't see it?"

"Because you weren't looking for it Nate, it's enchanted. Unless you are looking for it, you will never see it."

"So how did you find it?"

"Like I said Nate, the old fashioned way. When I walked into it I nearly knocked myself out, but there was nothing there. Looking again, I saw a small cobblestone wall. Realizing that the only cobblestone walls in the middle of the jungle are temple walls it suddenly materialized in front of me, just like it did for you."

"Ok, sort of makes sense, but how come Jethro was able to see it?"

"Quite simple Nathan, because I was looking for it."

"But why were you looking for something you did not even know was here? Argh, my head hurts."

"But Nathan, my boy, we did know it was here. In fact we all arranged to meet here, if you remember?"

"So this is the jungle temple we saw from on top of the cliff?"

"No"

"Argh, come on Jethro, this is killing me. Just tell me what's happening."

"Ok Nathan," laughs Jethro. "I'll put you out of your misery, this is a different temple to the one we have to meet Jay and Hailey at tomorrow, but it is a temple. So, as I am walking through the jungle I am conscious that we are searching for a temple, so when we came upon this enchanted temple I was able to see it. Understand now?"

"Not really, but I'll take your word for it. So Natasha, what's inside?"

"No idea."

"Why not?"

"Well Nate, as Jethro will tell you, temples usually contain hostile mobs, so I was waiting for reinforcements before going inside."

"If there are monsters in there, then why go inside?"

"Two reasons Nate, firstly, after we clear it out, we will have a secure place to rest tonight and secondly, temples nearly always contain treasure."

"Treasure, like what?"

"Like gold and diamonds and often, enchanted weapons."

"Cool, so do we split it three ways, is that the deal?

Laughing, Natasha and Jethro look at each other and shrug.

"Sure Nate, we split it three ways. You ready to explore the temple Indie?"

"Lead on Natasha, I'm feeling lucky."

Walking to the temple steps, they draw their swords and each light a torch. When fully prepared they walk in through the huge entrance into the darkness beyond, followed closely by Fawkes and Flumey.

★ ★ ★ ★ ★

Watching them searching the area around the tree, Warlord stays well back so is unable to hear Jay and Hailey's conversation, but quickly realizes what they are doing when he sees Jay bend and scoop up Jack's possessions. I wonder if they are sentimental or precious. Watching them leave and head deeper into the jungle, he creeps forward, and surveys the area. Looking up the cliff face, reviewing the damage the tree had caused on its downward descent he ponders whether Jack had fallen from above or if the tree had fallen on him. Probably fell, judging that the others were still up top when I stumbled on them. Rookie mistake, maybe that is why he was Jack the Dweeb, he chuckles. Giving the area one last sweep he heads off into the jungle, quietly following the trail left by Jay and Hailey.

★ ★ ★ ★ ★

"Which way Munster?"

"No idea boss, the trail just ends here."

"It can't just stop, not unless they knew we were following them."

"Don't know boss, but like you said earlier, they were expecting trouble of some sort so maybe this is their way of avoiding it."

"True. Ok, let's spread out and look for any signs of where they have gone, but keep your eyes peeled, this could be a trap."

Walking in opposite directions, they both move past the entrance to the temple that the others had just waked into less than an hour previously, and continue through the jungle looking for signs of their prey. Moving slowly and silently they part the foliage and push their way through, leaving no sign that they had passed.

I suppose they could have done the same, thinks PowerGlide. If so they will not be too far ahead of us, only trouble is we do not know what direction they travelled. Looking up into the canopy, way above his head, he notices that the shadows are getting longer and dusk is rapidly approaching. Heading back in the direction that he had just travelled he retraces his steps, but after a few minutes realizes that he is totally lost. Cursing he starts to cut a path back in the general direction he had just travelled, placing a torch here and there as the shadows lengthen, not wanting to get caught by any mobs spawning behind him.

Moving stealthily, Warlord makes good time, cutting only the branches necessary to allow him to move through the foliage. After travelling for some minutes, he realizes that there is absolutely no sign of his prey, so he turns and retraces his steps back to the trail, using the cut plants as a guide. Standing at the end of the trail there is no sign of PowerGlide, and no discernable clues as to where he has gone. Debating what to do next, he turns and walks one-step into the forest and bangs into a cobblestone wall.

What the hell? Running his hands along the 3 x 2 wall, he cannot think why anyone would build such a structure here in the forest. Removing his pickaxe, he starts to break the first block only to find another one behind it. Walking along the front of the wall, he looks behind it but can only see jungle, but looking back at the wall it is 2 blocks deep. Strangle, he thinks, and starts breaking a 2 block high hole in the wall. Deeper and deeper he digs until he has to stop and light a torch, then continues to break blocks. Stopping to take a break, he learns against the wall and looks back up the corridor. Must be 60 blocks deep and still nothing he thinks, when a shadow catches his eye, moving past the entrance. Putting his pickaxe away and drawing his sword he moves cautiously back up the corridor.

As he reaches the end, he can see a shadow moving around to his right, just out side of his line of vision. Taking a deep breath, he jumps from the cobblestone entrance and brings his sword around, ready to attack whatever is waiting for him. To his surprise, PowerGlide, who is also brandishing his sword, meets him.

"Bloody hell boss, you just scared the crap out of me."

"What the hell are you playing at Munster? I thought I told you to be quiet, and here you are making enough noise to let every mob in this jungle know where we are," but I am glad you did or I would have been lost for good, he thinks.

"Sorry boss, but I found this really weird wall," he replies pointing at the 3 x 2 cobblestone wall behind him.

"So, it's a cobblestone wall, no big deal."

"Yeah boss, but take a look behind it."

He peers over Munster's shoulder at a 3x2 cobblestone wall sat in the middle of the jungle. "So, it's a small wall, what's your point?"

"Now look at the hole I just dug."
"Munster, I don't have time to look through your hole in the wall, now what's going on?"

"Just humor me boss."

Shrugging, PowerGlide pushes Munster out of the way and looks into the hole he had dug and gasps. It is at least 60 blocks deep with torches burning along the walls. Stepping away from the opening, he once again looks at the wall but its still just 3x2 with forest behind it.

"What the hell?"

"I know, right?"

"How did you find this?"

"Walked into it boss, one minute it was jungle then I crashed my head against something and when I looked up there was this wall."

"I wonder?" smiles PowerGlide walking over to the wall and running his had along the blocks, but instead of stopping at the end he continues to run his hand and more blocks magically appear. Stepping back, he looks around with a big smile on his face.

"Well done, you know what you have found Munster?"

"A magic wall?"

"Use your head, and I don't mean to bash into it either."

"I don't know boss, it's just a wall."

"No, it's so much more. Instead of thinking of it as a wall think of it as a temple."

"Ah boss, you're making fun of me now, there's no way that this tiny little wall is a temple," turning to point at the wall his mouth drops open and he is lost for words as a huge temple is now stood in a clearing before him. "How the hell did that get there?"

"Ok Munster, you play this game, now it really is time to use your head. A temple magically appears in a jungle after you look for it, that would mean it's....?

Slapping his forehead, he replies, "of course boss, it's an enchanted temple. No wonder the trail ended, the others must have found it already."

"Exactly, now it's starting to get dark so let's get in there and seal ourselves in, then we can start the hunt for real."

"Nice, let's go."

Walking to the temple entrance, they quickly survey the area, and find footprints leading to a stonewall, and then disappearing.

"Looks like they are still being tracked by those big cats boss, but I don't know how they didn't notice them before they sealed themselves in."

"Maybe they went inside and looked around then came back to seal the entrance but the cats had already followed them?"

"Don't know boss, the footprints are everywhere, surely they would have noticed them?"

"Who knows Munster? Come on, let us take a quick look inside, and then seal it up before the mobs arrive. We'll worry about those cats if we find them in here."

Moving into the first room, they both light a torch and survey their surroundings.

"Nice boss, you think there is treasure in here."

"Guaranteed Munster. Only question is who will find it first."

"Doesn't matter who finds it, only matters who ends up with it," replies Munster running his thumb along the edge of his sword.

"Right you are, ok, let's seal this place up. I'll seal the entrance you check for any other passages, just leave the main one open, we can start there."

Moving forward as the sun dips below the tree line, PowerGlide places blocks of cobblestone across the entrance and plunges the temple into darkness, now lit only with the torches they carry. Moving around the room, he places torches at each corner and lights the place up.

"Right, you ready to hunt?"

"Always boss."

"Good, then let's bag ourselves some player's heads," he laughs, moving down the main tunnel.

✸ ✸ ✸ ✸ ✸

Shuffling through the jungle, the foliage heaves, and thousands of tiny feet move forward. Not a sound is heard above the smashing vegetation, but a wide corridor is created as thousands of creepers continue their march after their prey. Suddenly bursting out of the jungle they march forward, into the fast flowing river and are rapidly swept over the waterfall to the waiting mist below. Like lemmings, they continue this suicidal mission until they have all disappeared over the edge and peace once more descends on the jungle.

✸ ✸ ✸ ✸ ✸

"Come on Hailey, keep up. The temple can't be much further but we're loosing daylight."

"You keep going Jay, I'm going to hang here for a moment."

"Right, but don't rest too long, we only have about twenty minutes before we lose the sun."

"Ok Jay, I'll be right behind you."

Slipping quietly into the jungle foliage, she draws her bow and stares down the tunnel like trail they have left through the jungle foliage. After a minute, she hears something approaching stealthily. Notching an arrow and drawing her bow, she waits for whatever it is to come into range. Slowly, a fully armored figure appears along the trail and moves towards her, checking the ground at regular intervals.

Why you sneaky bastard, she thinks, aiming for the break in the armor between the leg and the hip. As the figure moves into range, she lets loose an arrow and rapidly fires a second. Hoping to predict where the figure will move.

✸ ✸ ✸ ✸ ✸

Moving along the jungle trail, Warlord bends down and examines the ground. Less than five minutes ahead of me now, he thinks, standing and continuing forward. Suddenly, from the jungle foliage ahead, an arrow fly's out and strikes him in the top of his leg, finding the narrow gap between his armor. Screaming in pain, he throws himself to the floor on his left as another arrow streaks by. Rolling to the edge of the jungle, he kneels and looks for an opponent. Another arrow shoots from the jungle and embeds itself in his shoulder. Bellowing in agony he jumps to his feet, turns and runs back down the rail, but not before another arrow finds a new home in the back of his leg. Limping out of range, he turns and spots a dark shape detach itself from the foliage and disappear up the trail.

Hobbling back along the trail for another 40 blocks he stops and makes sure he has not been followed then bends and snaps the arrow from his leg. Gritting his teeth against the pain, he reaches for the arrow in his leg. Even to touch this arrow is agony but he knows he will not be able to move properly unless he can remove it. Placing a twig between his teeth, he bites down hard and, with a determined tug, rips the arrow from his leg, passing out as he does so.

★ ★ ★ ★ ★

Running along the trail Hailey soon catches up with Jay.

"Where have you been? You can rest when we are at the temple."

"Sorry Jay, I thought I heard something following us so I wanted to check it out."

"Nothing there then?"

"Oh yeah, we were being followed by another player, but I think I have persuaded him to find somewhere else this evening."

Looking at Hailey with a smug smile on her lips, Jay asks, "go on then, don't leave me hanging."

"According to his name tag it was Wardlor999, you ever heard of him?"

"Yeah, he's a tricky bastard. Kills everything he meets, players or otherwise, but he's also got a good brain in his head."

"Well, he didn't look so clever running off with four arrows stuck in his armor."

"You got four arrows in him, nice work Hailey. There are not many people who could get the drop on Warlord and walk away to tell the tale."

"Ah, he's not so tough, if he hadn't had that iron armor he would be dead now."

"No doubt, so where did he go?"

"Last I saw he was hot tailing it back up the trail. I don't expect we will see him again tonight, but just in case I'll keep my eyes peeled."

"Nice work, I must admit I didn't even know he was there."

"That's ok Jay, you have other things on your mind, not to mention you're the one cutting the trail."

"Talking of which we better get a move on, look, you can see the top of the temple above the trees. Only about another 40 blocks."

Cutting for all he is worth, Jay slashes his way towards the temple while Hailey keeps her eyes peeled on the trail behind them, not really believing that Warlord would give up so easily. As dusk draws in on them, they burst out of the jungle into a wide-open clearing with a giant temple ruins in he middle.

"Right, no time to waste, up to the entrance, go." As they run across the clearing, Jay continues, "straight into the first room Hailey, it's usually a large anti chamber, if it's clear I want you to seal all the entrances and light some torches. I will seal the main entrance, once we have a secure area we'll make a plan."

They reach the stone steps and bound up them, two at a time. Slowing as they reach the top, they move cautiously into the temple and Jay lights two torches and throws one to Hailey. Taking a quick surveillance of the large empty room, they complete their tasks and seal not only the front entrance but also all tunnels leading from the room. Sitting on a block in the middle of the chamber, Hailey turns to Jay and asks.

"So, what now?"

Chapter 11

Game On

As darkness descends on the plateau, hundreds of zombies burst from the forest, pushing and shoving, racing for the steps cut into the side of the cliff face. They can smell their prey, and have been driven insane - at least more insane than they are already - waiting for the sun to set before they are able to pursue the fresh meat.

Reaching the jungle floor, the first of the zombies set off along the trail, with hundreds of their fellow meatheads in pursuit. They move relentlessly, even at a shuffle they cover the ground quite quickly and before long they reach the fallen tree. The first of the zombies mill around, following the scents left by their prey, they circle the tree a dozen times before one zombie finds the new trail and shuffles after the players. Before long, all the zombies are shuffling and rambling along the trail, groaning and moaning, sensing fresh meat up ahead.

★ ★ ★ ★ ★

Pulling themselves from the river, the creepers crawl up the bank next to the boats, and then move off along the sand and into the jungle. For many minutes the creepers continue to pour from the river, until just a few stragglers remain, who run after the others and disappear from sight, leaving thousands of small footprints in the sand.

*****

Waking some time later, Warlord looks around but can see very little. Rubbing his eyes he realizes that they are not the problem, darkness has descended while he has slept. Jumping to his feet, a sharp pain runs through his leg and he is reminded why he passed out. Reaching into his inventory, he removes some cooked pork and gobbles it down, immediately feeling his life points increase, and the pain in his leg diminishes. Quickly assessing the situation, he remembers what happened to him and grimaces. Drawing his sword, and a torch, he once again moves forward along the trail, keeping a careful eye out for any mobs that may spawn at any time.

Approaching the end of the trail, he can see a large clearing opening up at the far edge of his torch light. Moving into the clearing, the shadowy shape of jungle ruins comes into sight. So that is where they were heading, let's take a little look and see what they are up to. Turning quickly at the sound of moaning he spots a couple of zombies shuffling out of the forest at the other side of the clearing. Ah no, not more zombies. Rushing forward he slices both of their heads clean off and looks about to make certain that they are alone. Breathing deeply, he gives a sigh of relief, seeing nothing moving in the clearing.

Stealthily approaching the temple, he finds that it is completely sealed with cobblestone where the doors should be. So it looks like they are already inside. Guess I had better pay them a visit. Removing his pickaxe, he hammers away at the cobblestone until it breaks, only to find another one behind it. I wonder how many they put here, hammering at the next one until it too breaks he is shocked to find it is immediately replaced. What the crap? Hitting and smashing the block again, he gets a quick glimpse of someone inside lit chamber before the block is once again replaced. Digging furiously, he smashes the block, and prepares to smash the next one when an arrow shoots out of the opening and sticks him in his shoulder. Dropping the pickaxe and rolling to the side, he notices that not only is the block once again immediately replaced but also the outside block, completely sealing the wall.

Screaming in a mixture of pain and defiance, he rips the arrow from his shoulder and is about charge the wall when movement at the corner of his eye catches his attention. Glancing over, there are hundreds of zombies pouring into the clearing from the jungle trail he had just entered through. Momentarily stunned at the sight the first of the zombies are almost on him before he regains his wits and glancing around for an escape route. Shocked to see more zombies heading from all directions he realizes that there is no escape this time. There is no way to fight his way through hundreds of zombies. Swallowing, he takes one last look around and then stops. You stupid idiot. Quickly putting his sword away, he grabs some cobblestone from his inventory and places it underneath himself, jumping up and placing a second just as the first zombies reach him with arms outstretched, trying to grab him before he can escape. Quickly jumping again, he places another 3 blocks before he feels safe enough to pause and take stock of his situation.

There are hundreds, if not thousands of zombies, pushing and shoving in the clearing below him. OMG! I have never seen so many zombies."Hey meatheads," he shouts, "come and get me! ha, ha." Looking around for escape options, he nearly falls from his escape tower as an arrow hits him in the leg. Screaming, he pulls it out, and is looking to see where it came from as another shoots past his ear. Skeletons. Jumping up he quickly places another 10 blocks below him trying to get out of arrow range. 15 blocks, should be ok but I have no idea what the skeletons range is when shooting up. Quickly constructing a 3 x 4 platform to give him some protection from below he slumps to the floor and is pondering his situation when in a flash of light an enderman appears at the edge of the platform.

Endermen are 3 blocks tall, totally black, stick insect like creatures that have the ability to teleport. Unfortunately for Warlord, they also have the habit of stealing blocks, and making off with them. Although extremely dangerous, they usually do not engage in combat unless you make eye contact, at least Warlord hopes this is still the case in this mixed up minecraft world.

Diverting his eyes, so as not to antagonize it, he wonders briefly, what it is doing here, when it disappears carrying one of his cobblestone blocks with it. What the....., but before he can finish his curse it reappears, grabs another cobblestone block and disappears with it again.

Jumping to his feet, just as it reappears, he nearly loses his balance as the block below his feet is grabbed and suddenly vanishes, along with the enderman. Jumping to the edge of the platform he quickly replaces the missing blocks, just as the enderman reappears and once again grabs the block below his feet. Jumping to the side as the block vanishes, he quickly replaces it but realizes that he is fighting a losing battle. Just one mistake and the enderman will send him falling into the waiting hoards below. Making up his mind, just as the enderman reappears, he places a block at the edge of the platform and continues to build sideways towards the ruins. Running, placing blocks, and jumping he moves 5 blocks forward before the enderman grabs the block below his feet and sends him falling. Reaching out he grabs hold of the next block and manages to pull himself back onto the platform just as the enderman reappears. Realizing what is about to happen, Warlord jumps in the air and places a block below him just as the enderman grabs hold and disappears. It is too close to call, Warlord hovers in mid air, not knowing if the block he had just placed would stay or fall to the ground, throwing him into to the waiting arms of the zombies below him.

✴ ✴ ✴ ✴ ✴

The ocelot gives a deep throated growl, and and sniffs along the wall blocking the temple entrance.

"What's up Bluey?"

"Bluey, who's Bluey?" asks Jay.

"My ocelot, got to call her something and she's so dark grey that she's almost blue."

"True, good a name as any I suppose. Guess I had better name mine too. Hey, what's that noise?" asks Jay, looking up at the temple entrance.

"Sounds like digging."

"Yeah, well mobs don't dig so that means we have company."

Jumping to his feet, Jay draws his sword but Hailey stops him and tells him to get cobblestone instead. Looking a little bewildered, he does as she says, watching her draw her bow.

"Right, when the block breaks quickly place a new one in the opening, do it twice and then step aside."

Jay does exactly as instructed, and after replacing 2 blocks quickly jumps out of the way and Hailey steps up to the hole, draws her bow, and shoots an arrow at whoever is trying to gain entrance.

"Fill it in Jay," shouts Hailey, stepping aside.

Jumping back to the wall, Jay takes advantage of the situation, leans forward, and fills the outside and inside holes with cobblestone. Turning back to Hailey he is about to speak, but she shakes her head and looks back at the wall. They stand, waiting for another attempt but after a couple of minutes give a sigh of relief.

"So, did you see who it was?"

"Yeah, it was Warlord again, I guess he never got the message the first time, but I think that will be the last he bothers us."

"Why, you think you killed him with one arrow?"

"Nah, only got his shoulder but what I saw behind him should take care of the situation for us."

"Ok, I'll bite, what did you see behind him?"

"Only about a million zombies, that's what."

"Really, a million?"

"Well, maybe not quite a million, but certainly hundreds, and I don't care how good a fighter he is there is no way he can take on that many and live."

"I don't know Hailey, we did."

"Yeah, but we were ready for them. By the look on Warlord's face, he did not even know they were behind him. He doesn't stand a chance."

"Well, let's wait and see, if you're right we should hear a canon any time now."

Waiting in silence for five minutes, Hailey jumps to her feet. "We can't just sit here wondering, I'm going to open up a block and look outside."

"No!" Jay jumps up and grabs Hailey's arm as she picks up a pickaxe, "if I was him, I would have built a quick wall around me and I would now be waiting for some idiot to open a hole in the wall, and then guess what I would do?"

"Shoot an arrow through it?"

"Exactly, leave him be, he will either make it or he won't. If he tries to get in again we kill him, otherwise we wait for the morning."

"Right, sorry Jay."

"No problem, now let's get something to eat, how's your health points?"

"My health points?"

Looking up, Jay looks embarrassed. "Sorry, I forgot you're human, or rather I'm not human, but you are."

"No worries Jay, I'm so used to looking at blockmen that it does not even seem weird anymore."

"Right, so are you hungry?"

"Starving, what you got?"

"Pork, beef, and a little bread."

"Great, give me a beef sandwich."

Breaking the bread in half, Jay hands it to Hailey with a lump of cooked beef, "So, what's the plan? you want to wait here until morning or go explore a little?"

"Explore definitely, I'll go mad sat here, waiting to see if Warlord tries to get in again or not."

"Yeah me too, I know I said we should wait but the tunnels are still going to be dark whatever time of day we explore them and besides, we now have an early warning system," he smiles, pointing at the ocelots.

"Yeah cool. So what are you going to call your one Jay?"

"Stripes!"

"But it doesn't have any stripes?"

"Yeah I know, that's why it's a cool name," he laughs, but Hailey just stares at him with a blank expression. "Well Jack would have got it."

"I'm sorry Jay, I guess I'm not helping much, am I?"

"No but its ok Hailey, Jack's at home, I have to believe that or I will just go mad. Hey, where is Jack's ocelot, it's not here."

"Come to think of it I haven't seen it since Jack, uh, went home."

"No, nor me. I guess after Jack went home, the ocelot up and left."

"Makes sense, Jack tamed it, now he's gone the ocelot reverts to being wild. So, you ready to go?"

"As ready as I'll ever be, come on," he replies, grabbing a torch in one hand and his sword in the other. "Let's see if we can find some treasure."

Breaking down the cobblestone wall into the first tunnel, they both step inside and then Jay blocks it back up again.

✱ ✱ ✱ ✱ ✱

"So which way to you want to go Jethro?"

"Stick to the side tunnel on the left to start."

"I would have thought the main tunnel would be the obvious choice," states Nathan.

"You would think so, but in my experience the main tunnel always has traps, and there's no more chance of treasure than any other tunnel. We can start here then we can always explore the others afterwards. Nate you block the other tunnels and I will seal the temple entrance. Right, you guys ready for some treasure hunting?"

They both nod to Jethro's question and set off down the side tunnel, closely followed by Fawkes and Flumey. Moving deeper into the temple they pass many empty rooms until they get to a large, wooden door, blocking the way forward.

"Careful Natasha, just take it slow and easy. You know as well as I do that these places are always full of traps."

"Chill Jethro, I know what I'm doing."

As Natasha reaches her hand towards the door, Flumey and Fawkes start to growl, the hair standing up on the backs of their necks.

"Keep your pets quite guys, we don't know what's behind the door, and we sure as hell don't want to alert it that we are here."

Looking at the ocelots, Nathan smiles, then moves up to Natasha and whispers, "I think they are trying to tell us there's something in the room. Look at them," he points at the ocelots that are pacing backwards and forwards, growling and bearing their teeth. "There's definitely something in there Natasha."

Looking at Nate, then back at the ocelots she replies. "You know what, you could be right. So Jethro, what do we do?"

"Right, I say two of us throw open the doors, with swords drawn ready for any mobs, while the other has cobblestone ready to block the opening if we are confronted by something more than we bargained for.

What do you say Nathan, sword or cobblestone?"

"I'll take a sword, remember, I've seen you fight Jethro and it's not a pretty picture."

"I would disagree with you dear boy, but alas, I'm afraid you are correct."

"So where have all the gentlemen gone?" asks Natasha. "So much for chivalry, I'm surprised at you Jethro."

"Really Natasha, you know very well that you are our best bet in any armed confrontation."

"Yeah I know, I just like to hear you say it," she smiles, winking at Nathan.

"Right, so all agreed, on the count of three, myself, and Nathan will open the doors, throw in a torch and you Natasha, get ready to defend."

"Agreed," they both reply.

Putting their shoulders to the doors and pushing them open, they both throw a lit torch through the opening and stand aside. Nathan, with sword in hand and Jethro with cobblestone. Tensing her muscles, Natasha readies herself for an assault by hostile mobs but is slightly disappointed when nothing happens. Looking at each other, they move cautiously into the room. It is a large open chamber, about 40 x 30, with a large glowing pit in the middle. Indicating that Jethro should stay by the door, Natasha moves along the left wall, while Nathan circles along the right. They both make it to the far side of the room, then move towards the pit in the centre. Arriving at the edge of the 5 x 5 opening, they quickly assess the situation.

"You ok Nate?"

"Sure, so what is it?" he asks, pointing at the pedestal with a chest on top, surrounded by lava.

"It's a temple, so I guess this is an alter, or something."

"Ok, but what does it do?"

"Nothing, or rather it's probably a test with some sort of prize in that chest.

"Cool, so how do we get it?"

"Watch out."

Spinning as Jethro shouts a warning, Natasha comes face to face with a large spider descending from the ceiling. Swinging her sword, she cuts at the spider's legs as another drops to the floor beside her. Backpedaling furiously she continues to chop away, killing the first spider and defending against the second as more spider drop on her from above.

Spotting a spider approaching Natasha from behind, Nathan jumps into the battle and chops at it before it can strike. Cutting it clean in two, he stands back to back with Natasha and defends against the next spider that attacks.

"Thanks Nate, just keep them away from my back and I'll take care of business."

Jumping forward she slices the eyes on a spider that has just landed on the floor and with a backswing takes the legs off the next. Grunting with exhaustion, she continues to chop away at their assailants as Nathan defends her rear, killing another as it tries to attack him from above.

As more spider descend on glowing webs, Nathan shouts. "There's too many, we can't defend against this many."

"Who's defending? Attack them Nathan, cut them up." Turning to Jethro, she shouts, "a little help Jethro, if you're not too busy."

Feeling a little foolish, standing in the doorway with cobblestone in his hands, watching his friends fight, he quickly draws his sword and dashes into the melee. Swinging wildly, with little precision, it is amazing how much damage he inflicts on the spiders. Legs fly everywhere, and soon they finish off the last of them.

Looking over at Jethro, Natasha raises her eyebrows. "That was quite an impressive display for someone who said they can't fight."

"Well, I quite impressed myself. Simply swinging like a mad man and spinning in circles seems to work a treat on spiders," he replies with a huge smile plastered on his face.

"Nice work J-Dog."

"J-Dog?" asks Natasha.

"Yeah, J-Dog. He may be old but he's one of us, isn't that right Jethro."

"Yes Nathan, I most certainly am."

As Nathan wanders back over to the pit, Natasha looks over at Jethro and asks, "just how old are you?"

"Well I'm ...."

A ball of lava shoots out of the lava straight at Nathan's head. Diving to the side, he rolls and kneels up, waiting to see what happens next. When nothing further happens, he looks to Natasha and Jethro, who both shrug, and edge closer to him.

"What was that?"

"No idea Nate. How about you Jethro?"

"Hm, I wonder. Nate, do you think you can do that again?"

"What, get a lava ball thrown at me?"

"Yes, exactly that, I'm going to go around the other side and watch what happens when you approach the pit again."

"Are you mad? That thing almost killed me."

"Hardly Nathan, it did not even touch you. Right, if you would just wait for me to get in position, then approach the pit again, and please try and keep your head down." Walking around the side of the room, he moves to the far side of the pit and removes something from his inventory. "Ok, when you're ready."

Looking at Natasha, Nathan asks. "He's serious right? He wants me to get another ball of lava thrown at me so he can watch."

"Yep, I'm just glad he asked you and not me. Now Nate, off you go. Listen to J-Dog and keep your head down," she laughs.

"Yeah, yeah, real funny," he replies moving ever so carefully towards the pit. When nothing happens, he rises and walks along the edge. Turning to Natasha, he says. "Nothing, maybe I stepped on a trap or something the first time."

"Down Nathan," shouts Jethro as another flaming ball shoots out of the pit straight at Nathan's head.

Ducking just in time he rubs his hair as it starts to ignite from the heat, as the flaming ball shoots past him

Stepping forward as he shouts, Jethro raises the bucket that he had removed from his inventory and empties the water onto the lava monster that has risen out of the lava. In a hiss of steam, the lava monster gives a thunderous crack and falls apart.

Rushing to the side of the pit, Natasha and Nathan watch as the lava monster turns to obsidian and sinks below the surface.

"What was that?"

"That Nathan was a lava monster."

"A lava monster, I've never seen one of them before."

"Well they are not that common Natasha. Only if you are playing on a server with that mod pack added would you have ever encountered one."

"But how did you know they were here. There weren't any announcements."

"Quite, Jay and myself were discussing that very point just before we lost the village to the creepers. We think that the announcement for 'The Infection' mod pack was more likely a blanket announcement that all mod packs are now in play."

"Really, and you never thought to mention it to anyone?"

"No, I guess what with running from the creepers, then escaping down the river, taming ocelots and falling over a waterfall to come and find you, that it simply slipped my mind."

"Oh right, sorry, I guess we have been a little busy."

"Yes, quite alright Natasha. So, what now then?"

"Now we get ourselves some treasure," shouts Nathan, jumping up and high fiving Natasha.

✴ ✴ ✴ ✴ ✴

Landing on the block, Warlord gives a huge sigh of relief, then immediately starts laying blocks in the direction of the temple. The enderman reappears behind him and grabs the block below his feet, but Warlord is ready for him and jumps up, placing a block below him and continuing to build. He is within 2 blocks of the temple when the enderman reappears and grabs the block below his feet, too quick for him this time, all he can do is throw himself forward and hope for the best.

Landing on the edge of the temple, he grabs hold of the block as his legs swing over the edge. The zombies below surge forward, sensing that they will be able to feed shortly. Grunting, Warlord quickly pulls himself up onto the temple and rolls a few blocks away from the edge, just as the enderman reappears and steals the block that he was just holding on to. Safely away from the edge he breaths a sigh of relief just as the enderman reappears. Standing 3 blocks high, he wavers in front of him, looking at the temple then back at Warlord again. Trying to watch the enderman without making direct eye contact, he wonders what it's up to when in a flash it's gone again. Jumping to his feet, prepared to run if it appears again he waits, tense and unsure of what's happening. After a few minutes, he starts to relax as he realizes that the enderman has given up. There are far too many blocks in the temple to steal to make it worth the effort. Surveying the immediate temple surroundings, he discovers that he is over 12 blocks straight down to the ground at the lowest point. No way can any zombies get up that, and the enderman would have one hell of a job stealing blocks to make a staircase without him noticing. Deciding that his best option is to make a defensive position here and wait for daybreak he immediately builds a 6 x 6 wall, 2 blocks high using cobblestone, just in case the zombies get to the top of the temple somehow. Placing torches at each corner of the wall, he sits on the top and eats the last of his cooked pork while watching the zombies shuffling about below him.

★ ★ ★ ★ ★

Moving stealthily along the main tunnel PowerGlide and Munster look for traps, or any sign of mobs. Passing two empty rooms, Munster stops and indicates that PowerGlide should come over to him. Whispering in his ear, he says, "no sign of anything boss, no mobs and no players, I think they must have gone down one of the other tunnels."

"You're probably right, so what do you want to do, explore a little further or head back and try to find them?"

"I say head back boss, this place creeps me out."

"Yeah, you're not wrong there Munster."

Turning, they start back up the tunnel but stop and crouch when they get to the bend, hearing voices ahead of them. Smiling wicked smiles and nodding to one another they prepare to attack whoever is around the bend in the corridor. Jumping out, screaming their war cry they are shocked to find it empty. Twirling swiftly to check the rear, they find they are totally alone.

"What the... where are they?"

"Listen boss."

Settling down they listen to sounds coming from just ahead.

"You think they're around the next bend?"

"No boss, I think these tunnels are playing tricks on us. I bet they are all the way back up at the anti-chamber where we came in."

"You could be right, come on, let's get them before they get away."

Running back up the corridor, slowing to check around each bend, they make good time and quickly make it back to the tunnel entrance. Seeing shadows moving in the large anti-chamber, they slow their advance, nod to each other and burst out of the corridor with swords raised high above their heads, ready to strike their enemies.

★ ★ ★ ★ ★

"Ok, let's build a platform across to the chest and see what treasure we have found."

"Slow down Nate, there could be more of those lava monsters in there," warns Natasha.

"Nah, it would have attacked by now. What do you think Jethro?"

"You are probably correct Nathan, but just in case I will stand here, ready with my last bucket of water."

"Ok cool, so what's the plan Natasha?"

"Build a cobblestone platform, 3 blocks wide over to the chest, then take a look and see if it's all kosher."

"Why 3 blocks wide, isn't that just wasting time?"

"No Nate, this is minecraft, and as you may have noticed, there are plenty of things that will quite happily kill you, so you always have to be careful. Building a 3 block wide platform will give me a clear block to either side and behind, if I need to get out of trouble."

"Cool, but why are you going over, not me?"

Sighing, Natasha continues, "ok Nate, how many treasure chests have you found and opened in minecraft? hmm, what is that, I cannot hear you? oh right, none. In fact you have never even played minecraft, so before you get all cocky just stand back and watch someone who knows what she is doing and maybe you will learn something."

Crestfallen, Nathan watches Natasha carefully move across the platform. Walking to his side, with his bucket of water ready, Jethro learns over and whispers.

"Cheer up Nathan, she is right. You are new here and she's only looking out for you."

"I know Jethro, but she's always saving me, I just want to help."

"You are dear boy and you are doing fine. Now keep your eyes open."

Watching Natasha advance across the platform, they hold their breath as she reaches the chest and reaches out her hand to open it. Slowly she feels around the edge of the lid, looking for any obvious traps, but feeling nothing she swallows, holds her breath and slowly raises the lid.

Silence. No explosions, no monsters jumping out and attacking, nothing. Letting out a great sigh of relief she looks over her shoulder and winks at Nathan, before looking into the chest. Lying on the bottom are two shapes in small sacks. Lifting the first sack from the chest she turns and throws it to Nathan, who catches it and puts it in his inventory, keeping his sword drawn, ready to defend Natasha. Looking back into the chest, she reaches for the second sack then pauses, reaches into her inventory and removes a long pole. Standing away from the chest, she jumps up and places 2 blocks under her, giving enough height to still see into the bottom of the chest. Reaching out with the pole, she snags the last sack and lifts it from the chest. Immediately the chest explodes and throws all three of them to the floor. Pulling himself to his feet, Nathan dusts himself off, checks on Jethro, who is fine, and looks around for Natasha.

"Natasha, where are you?" he shouts, fearing that she had been killed in the explosion.

"Over here Nate."

Running to the other side of the pit, he finds Natasha, lying against the wall.

"How did you get all the way over here?"

"When the chest blew, it caught me before I could move, but it must have been designed to kill anyone who stood in front of it because I felt all the shrapnel rush past below me, then the after shock picked me up and threw me over here."

"Are you ok?"

Patting herself all over, she looks up at Nathan and smiles, "yep, no damage done, and that Nate is how you open a chest in a temple."

Slapping his hand against his forehead and groaning, Nathan puts out his other hand and helps Natasha up.

"Remind me to let you open all the chests we find in future, seeing as you are soooo good at it."

Slapping him on the back of the head and laughing, Natasha replies, "oh very funny. So it did not go exactly to plan but as least no one got hurt, and we got the treasure."

"The treasure!" shouts Nathan, quickly withdrawing the bag from his inventory.

"Hold on Nate, let's not be too hasty. Put the bag on the floor, over there, and we will open it with a stick, ok."

Remembering what just happened, Nathan places the sack on the floor and steps out of the way. "You're right Natasha, you want to do the business?"

"Men!" she laughs. Pulling another pole from her inventory she pries open the sack and out rolls a diamond. "All clear," she says happily, and Nathan runs over and opens the sack all the way.

"Wow, there's 6 diamonds in here."

"Cool Nate, now let's see what's in the other sack."

Placing the last sack on the floor, she repeats the process and opens it using a long pole. When nothing happens, she looks at Nathan and nods, and he dashes forward and withdraws a large black ball from the bag.

"What's this?" he asks turning to Natasha.

"Oh cool Nate, looks like an Ender Pearl."

"What's an Ender Pearl?"

"Well, it's a pearl from The Nether region."

"Ok, I'll bite, what's The Nether region?"

"Ok, really simple lesson, we're in the Overworld, which includes everything in this world, including mines, oceans, etc. ok, so far?"

"Yep, keep going."

"Good, now there are other regions in minecraft and an Ender Pearl comes from a region called The Nether, I suppose it's based very loosely on our images of hell. All fiery lava fields, with ghasts and pigmen."

"And they are...?"

"Ok, ghasts are like ghosts that throw flame balls at you and pigmen are just as they sound. Men with pig heads. Hey, maybe they're just men, seeing as most men are pigheaded anyway."

"Ha,ha Natasha."

"Yes, very droll my dear, but I would like to point out that not all men are pigs."

"Sorry Jethro, I know that, it really was just a joke. Anyway, pigmen are cool and won't attack you unless you upset them somehow."

"Right, so this pearl thingy comes from The Nether, is it worth anything?"

"Absolutely! You can use it to build a teleporter, either to The Nether or just for teleportation. Here, let me show you," reaching out her hand she takes the Ender Pearl from Nathan and throws it across the room. As it rolls to a stop, she winks at him then immediately disappears and reappears standing over the Ender Pearl. Turning to look at Nathan, she smiles, "neat huh?"

"Wow, let me try," squeals Nathan, running across the room to

Natasha. Reaching out his hands to grab the Ender Pearl, she pulls it away from him and responds.

"No, my precious!"

"What?"

"Just joking, but in all seriousness Nate, you really have to be careful. Wherever you throw this, when it stop moving, you will be teleported there. Just imagine if it rolls into the lava, before you can stop it you will be teleported with it and its hello crispy fried Nate."

Gulping, imagining that scenario, he reaches for the Ender Pearl, "ok Natasha, I get it." Taking it from her outstretched hand, he gingerly tosses it 5 blocks along the edge of the room. The moment it stops rolling he is instantly teleported to its position. "Way cool, you can't even feel anything. One second you're here, the next there."

"Yes Nathan, used carefully it's a great asset. Now I suggest we get out of this chamber before any other nasties appear."

Looking at Nathan, Natasha mouths at him, 'Nasties! Where does this guy come from?'

Smiling at Natasha over his shoulder, Nathan walks up to Jethro, throws his arm over his shoulders and replies. "Yeah J-Dog, let's clear out, now that all the treasure is safely in our possession."

Putting his bucket of water back into his inventory, Jethro picks up his other bucket and bends over the pit, fills the bucket with lava and places it in his inventory. Turning, he finds both his friends staring at him with open mouths.

"What?"

"You just stuck a bucket of lava inside of you."

"Yes, of course. I do it all the time in minecraft."

"Yeah, but its one thing carrying water. What's the worst that can happen, wet pants, but lava?"

"Oh, I see what you are saying. I must confess I did not even think about it, I just filled the bucket because I thought it could be useful later."

"Big cahonies J-Dog. Way big cahonies," smiles Natasha.

Smiling despite himself, Jethro replies, "why thank you Natasha. I don't think anyone has ever made that particular remark about me before."

"Well I guess they don't really know you then. Ok people, let's move out."

Walking out the door, they head back up the tunnel towards the anti-chamber where they had entered, followed by their trusty friends, Flumey and Fawkes.

★ ★ ★ ★ ★

Settling in for the evening, Warlord stares out at the mass of zombies surrounding the temple, and wonders what will happen at daybreak. Obviously, they must have hidden during the day or there could never be that many of them here now, but will they hide again? Standing and stretching he spots the enderman standing at the edge of the tree line, looking at him hiding on the side of the temple. Immediately averting his eyes he is shocked to see another enderman on the other side of the clearing. Looking more carefully, he spots at least another three amongst the zombie hoards and is sure that there could be two or three more in the forest. Oh great, what have I gotten myself into now. Deciding that there is nothing he can do until daylight, he hunkers down in his temporary structure and prays that the endermen do not attack together, or he will have no blocks left hide behind.

★ ★ ★ ★ ★

Moving along the tunnel Jay and Hailey find many open doors with empty rooms behind. After searching the tenth room, Jay turns to Hailey and asks."So, you want to keep going? Looks like this place was cleaned out a long time ago."

"Yeah Jay, we may as well. There's nowhere we can go until morning anyway."

"Fair enough, how about we search until we reach the end of this passage, then head back to the anti-chamber for the night."

"Ok, sounds good."

Continuing to follow the passage, they pass another twelve empty rooms before reaching a set of double doors at the end.

"Right, let's take a quick look in here and get the hell out of here."

"Ok, you open the door Jay, I'll cover you with my bow."

Pushing open the door and jumping back out of the way, Jay stumbles and falls to the floor. Desperately trying to pull his sword, while backpedaling, he is starting to panic when Hailey says, "cool it Jay, it's empty, just calm down."

Looking up, he sees Hailey with her hand outstretched, ready to help him up. Sheepishly he grabs her offered hand and pulls himself to his feet.

"Sorry Hailey, I guess all the excitement has gotten to me. When I could not get my sword free, I imagined mobs attacking and started to panic."

"No need to apologies Jay, now, let's take a look and see what we have inside."

Walking into the room, with her bow drawn ready, Hailey checks behind the doors, and moves around the large room. Finding it empty, she lowers her bow.

"Nothing, I really thought we would find something in the old temple."

"Nah. Like I said, looks like it has been cleaned out a long time ago. Let's get out of here," Jay replies walking from the room, heading back up the corridor, as they had agreed. Looking over his shoulder, Jay finds he is alone, and backtracks to the room where he finds Hailey studying the ceiling, "hello, earth to Hailey, come in Hailey."

"Uh, what?"

"You coming girl, I thought we had finished here?"

"Take a look at the ceiling Jay, see how the wall reaches 6 blocks up to the beams over there but only 5 blocks here."

"Yeah, so?"

"So, that means whoever built this room is either a very bad architect or..."

"Yeah, or what?"

"Or...there is something blocked off behind this wall," she replies tapping on the higher wall.

"Ok, so let's find out," replies Jay removing his pickaxe from his inventory. "You watch my back, ok?"

"Of course Jay, anything comes out of the hole in the wall will be wearing arrows in its head."

"Nice image Hailey, real nice."

Breaking a 2 x 2 opening Jay stands back, lights a torch and throws it through the hole. It bounces off the back wall and comes to rest on the floor, lighting a narrow chamber, only 2 blocks wide, running the width of the room. As Jay is peering inside, Natasha asks. "Come on Jay, what's in there?"

Turning with a huge smile on his face he replies, "Dragon Eggs!"

★ ★ ★ ★ ★

Walking into the anti-chamber, Jethro, Natasha and Nathan sit in the lit room and Natasha removes three pieces of cooked pork from her inventory.

"Look's like that's all I have left. You guys got any more food?"

Looking, Jethro replies, "two pieces of pork and three loaves of bread, that is all. How about you Nathan?"

"I have two pieces of pork, that's it."

"Ok people, looks like we are going to have to do some shopping tomorrow."

"Yeah, just nip down to Wal-Mart will you Natasha, and grab some supplies," laughs Nathan.

Smiling, she replies, "Oh that would be so nice, I'd start with a huge burger and fries and finish with a whole gallon of ice cream."

"Yeah, but don't forget to grab some Mexican for me, burritos would hit the mark. How about you Jethro? Hey Jethro, you still with us?"

Looking up, Jethro smiles, and gets to his feet, "yes Nathan, some food would be lovely but I think we may have visitors."

"What?" shouts Natasha as she and Nathan both jump to their feet, drawing their swords, looking around the room, all is quite except for a faint snoring from Flumey and Fawkes, who are asleep already.

"You sure Jethro, I don't see anything and surely the ocelots would have warned us if there was anyone close."

"Hm, maybe, but I heard voices. I think we should be ready, just in case."

"Ok, which direction did they come from?"

"From the main tunnel over there," he points.

"Jethro, didn't we block that before we went down the other tunnel?"

"Yes, I think we did."

"Ok people, defensive positions," instructs Natasha as a blood-curdling war cries scream out of the tunnel. Immediately preparing for attack they wait, and wait. Looking at each other, Natasha shrugs, and hefts her sword, ready for whoever is moving along the tunnel.

"Sounds like two of them, both players, and they are obviously hunting us," states Jethro. "Maybe we should move out, rather than confronting them as we can't win anyway."

"Speak for yourself Jethro, I'm more than capable of defending myself," snaps Natasha.

"No Natasha, you don't understand, when a player attacks another player, they both lose an equal number of health points on each attack, so if you are both on full points you will both die. The only way to win is to start with more health points than your opponent."

"Or, all attack the same person," jumps in Nathan.

"What? And you are only telling me this now. Don't you think this is information that I should have had earlier?"

"Yes, of course, same excuse as earlier, no time now. I think we should make a hasty retreat while we still can."

"But there are three of us and you said two of them, I say let's stand and fight."

"Too risky. If they both gang up on one of us then that person is dead, no two ways about it. Come on Natasha, we can fight another time, on our own terms."

Looking at Jethro, then at Nathan, she nods and walks to the blocked up entrance to the temple, "ok, you win this time Jethro, but you two," she points at each in turn, "are going to sit down with me and have a very serious conversation when we get out of here."

Looking sheepishly at each other, both Jethro and Nathan nod and move to the temple entrance wall.

Removing his pickaxe, Jethro knocks a 2 x 2 hole in the wall just as PowerGlide and Munster come charging into the room, screaming their war cries with swords raised above their heads.

Looking at each other, Jethro, Natasha, and Nathan back out through the hole with swords raised in front of them. Calling for Fawkes and Flumey to follow, Nathan leans in through the hole and smiles at PowerGlide and Munster, then shouts, "later guys. Just stay here and you won't get hurt."

Lowering his sword, PowerGlide looks at Munster and chuckles. "Well well, that was easier than I thought."

"Yeah boss, let's just sit this one out," laughs Munster.

Backing all the way through the hole, Jethro quickly blocks it with cobblestone, turns to Natasha, and says, "that went rather well, I never really expected them to give up so easily."

Turning, Nathan stutters, "uh guys, you may want to take a look at this."

Turning together, Natasha and Jethro look out over the temple clearing and gasp in shock at the sight of thousands of creepers stood silently before them.

✱ ✱ ✱ ✱ ✱

Chapter 12

Notch Vs Herobrine

Waking in darkness, Notch is momentarily confused. Rubbing his eyes with the back of his hands, he looks around the cell and his recent memories flood his all ready overloaded brain. Jumping to his feet he grabs the cell doors, and finds them unlocked. Moving swiftly into the next room, he surveys his surroundings. It is a large chamber with six cells running off it and a heavy wooden door. No sign of Herobrine. Quickly checking the other cells, he finds them empty and moves to the heavy door. Opening it, he peers into the corridor beyond, which is also empty. Strange, why bother putting me in a cell if it is not locked. Cautiously moving along the corridor, he comes to a junction with passages going either direction. A sign hangs on the wall with arrows pointing each way. To the left is the Armory, to the right the Dining room. Choosing to go left, he edges along the corridor until he reaches a heavy, ironclad wooden door. Lifting the handle and pushing hard the door slowly swings inward to reveal a room full of weapons. Smiling to himself, he advances into the room and closes the door behind him.

Moving over to a display of swords, he grabs the closest one and ties the scabbard to his belt. He next grabs some knives, a bow, and a deadly looking axe. Moving further into the room, he finds himself in the armor section and admires a beautiful suit of diamond armor. What the hell, might as well have the best. Grabbing the diamond suit, he spots his reflection and stops dead.

- Finally, you take a long time to catch on Notch.

Hearing Herobrine's voice, he swings around and draws the sword, ready to fight for his freedom, but the room is empty.

- Behind you Notch.

Swinging around, he brings his sword down on a suit of armor, knocking it to the ground.

- Come now Notch, seeing that you designed this game you really are a little slow.

Spinning around he hunts wildly for his opponent, but is unable to locate him.

-So Notch, are you ready to talk?

"I will if you show yourself."

- Walk over to the mirror.

"What trick is this?"

- No trick Notch, just walk over to the mirror and all will be revealed.

Cautiously moving across the room, looking for traps, Notch arrives at the mirror, and asks. "So, now what?"

- Look Notch.

Turning, he looks in the mirror and is shocked to see his reflection. Staring back is a blocky character that slightly resembles himself, apart from the glowing white eyes.

- As I said Notch, we are one. Now let the games begin.

★ ★ ★ ★ ★

Here ends the second book in the Masters of Minecraft Series.

Book 3 - will be available in March 2014.

CPSIA information can be obtained at www.ICGtesting.com
Printed in the USA
LVOW13s1805170714

394812LV00021B/1317/P